MW01093358

A SILO STORY
SECOND SHIFT
ORDER

BY HUGH HOWEY

Second Shift:
Order

Edited by David Gatewood, Gay Murrill, and Dr. Amber Lyda
Cover design by Mike Tabor
Interior design and layout by Hugh Howey
Beta Readers: Jill Martin Clements, Jason Snyder,
Travis Mohrman, Holly Bryan, Brent Rendel, Moriah

ISBN-13: 978-148105-655-7
ISBN-10: 1-48105655-7

www.hughhowey.com

Give feedback on the book at:
hughhowey@gmail.com
Twitter: @hughhowey

Printed in the U.S.A

For those we terrify at birth.

• Silo 18 •

In the year of the Great Uprising

Now they lay me in the deep,
I pray the 'Lo my soul to keep.
To keep me safe inside the earth.

And if I die before I wake,
I pray the 'Lo my soul to take.
To take and grant another birth.

-Sasha Sway, age 11

Deathdays were birthdays. That's what they said to ease their pain, those who were left behind. An old man dies and a lottery is won. Children weep while hopeful parents cry tears of joy. Deathdays were birthdays, and no one knew this better than Mission Jones.

Tomorrow was his seventeenth. Tomorrow, he would grow a year older. It would also mark seventeen years since his mother died.

The cycle of life was everywhere—it wrapped around all things like the great spiral staircase—but nowhere was it more evident, nowhere could it be seen so clearly that a life given was one taken away. And so Mission approached his birthday without joy, with a heavy load on his young back, thinking on death and celebrating nothing.

Three steps below him and matching his pace, Mission could hear his friend Cam wheezing from his half of the load. When Dispatch assigned them a tandem, the two boys had flipped a coin, heads for heads, and Cam had lost. That left Mission with a clear view of the stairs. It also gave him rights to set the pace, and dark thoughts made for an angry one.

Traffic was light on the stairwell that morning. The children were not yet up and heading to school, those of them who still went anymore. A few bleary-eyed shopkeepers staggered toward work. There were service workers with grease stains on their bellies and patches sewn into their knees coming off late shifts. One man descended bearing more than a non-porter should, but Mission was in no mood to set down his burden and weigh another's. It was enough to glare at the gentleman, to let him know that he'd been seen.

"Three more to go," he huffed to Cam as they passed the twenty-fourth. His porter's strap was digging into his shoulders, the load a great one. Heavier still was its destination. Mission hadn't been back to the farms in near on four months, hadn't seen his father in just as long. His brother, of course, he saw at the Nest now and then, but it'd still been a few weeks. To arrive so near to his birthday would be awkward, but there was no helping it. He trusted his father to do as he always had and ignore the occasion altogether, to ignore that he was getting any older.

Past the twenty-fourth they entered another gap between the levels full of graffiti. The noxious odor of home-mixed paint hung in the air. Recent work dribbled in places, parts of it done the night before. Bold letters wrapped across the curving wall of concrete far beyond the stairway railing that read:

This is our 'Lo.

The slang for silo felt dated, even though the paint was not yet dry. Nobody said that anymore. Not for years. Farther up and much older:

Clean this, Mother-

The rest was obscured in a slap of censoring paint. As if anyone could read it and not fill in the blank on their own. It was the first half that was a killing offense, anyway. The second was just a word.

Down with the Up Top!

Mission laughed at this one. He pointed it out to Cam. Probably painted by some kid born above the mids and full of self-loathing, some kid who couldn't abide their own good fortune. Mission knew the kind. They were *his* kind. He studied all this graffiti painted over last year's graffiti and all the many years before. It was here between the levels, where the steel girders stretched out from the stairwell to the cement beyond, that such slogans went back generations. Atop the angry words were pockmarks, scars, and burns of old wars. Atop these wounds lay ever more angry scribbles, on and on.

The End is Coming . . .

Mission marched past this one, unable to argue. The end *was* coming. He could feel it in his bones. He could hear it in the wheezing rattle of the silo with its loose bolts and its rusty joints, could see it in the way people walked of late with their shoulders up around their ears, their belongings clutched to their chests. The end was coming for certain.

His father would laugh and disagree, of course. Mission could hear his old man's voice from all the levels away, could hear his father telling him how people had thought the same thing long before he and his brother were born, that it was the hubris of each generation to think this anew, to think that their time was special, that all things would come to an end with them. His father said it was *hope* that made people feel this, not dread. People talked of the end coming with barely concealed smiles. Their prayer was that when they went, they wouldn't go alone. Their hope was that no one would have the good fortune to come after.

Thoughts such as these made Mission's neck itch. He held the hauling strap with one hand and adjusted the 'chief around his neck with the other. It was a nervous habit, hiding his neck when he thought about the end of things. But that had been two birthdays ago.

"You doing okay up there?" Cam asked.

"I'm fine," Mission called back, realizing he'd slowed. He gripped his strap with both hands and concentrated on his pace, on his job. There was a metronome in his head from his shadowing days, a tick-tock, tick-tock for tandem hauls. Two porters with good timing could fall into a rhythm and wind their way up a dozen flights, never feeling a heavy load. Mission and Cam weren't there yet. Now and then one of them would have to shuffle his feet or adjust his pace to match the other. Otherwise, their load might sway dangerously.

Their load.

Mission's grandfather came to mind, though Mission had never known the man. He had died in the uprising of '78, had left behind a son to take over the farm and a daughter to become a chipper. Mission's aunt had quit that job a few years back; she no longer banged out spots of rust and primed and painted raw steel like she used to. Nobody did. Nobody bothered. But his father was still farming that same plot of soil, that same plot generations of Jones boys had farmed, forever insisting that things would go on, that they would never change.

"That word means something else, you know," his father had told him once, when Mission had spoken of revolution. "It also means to go around and around. To revolve. One revolution, and you get right back to where you started."

This was the sort of thing Mission's father liked to say when the priests came to bury a man beneath his corn. His dad would pack the dirt with a shovel, say that's how things go, and plant a seed in the neat depression his thumb made.

A few weeks later, Mission had told his friends this other meaning of revolution. He had pretended to come up with it himself. It was just the sort of pseudo-intellectual nonsense they regaled each other with late at night on dark landings while they inhaled potato glue out of plastic bags.

His best friend Rodny had been the only one unimpressed. "Nothing changes until we *make* it change," he had said with a serious look in his eye.

Mission wondered what his best friend was doing now. He hadn't seen Rodny in months. Whatever he was shadowing for on thirty-four kept him from getting out much.

He thought back to better days, growing up in the Nest with friends tight as a fist. He remembered thinking they would all stay together and grow old in the Up Top. They would live along the same hallways, watch their eventual kids play the way they had.

But all had gone their separate ways. It was hard to remember who had done it first, who had shaken off the shadowing expected by their parents, but eventually most of them had. Like a group decision never discussed, like a dozen private revolutions. They had left home to choose a new fate. Sons of plumbers took up farming. Daughters of the cafe learned to sew. None of them bothered to ask how many of their parents had done the same. Everything felt new and unique, and so it had to be.

Mission remembered being angry when he left home. He remembered a fight with his father, throwing down his shovel, promising he'd never dig a trench again. He'd learned in the Nest that he could be anything he wanted, that he was in charge of his own fate. And so when he grew miserable, he assumed it was the farms that made him feel that way; he assumed it was his family.

He thought about his mother, about family he had never known, and a ring of fire burned around his neck, the remnants of a rope's embrace.

He and Cam had flipped a dime back in Dispatch, heads for heads, and now Mission could feel a man's shoulders pressed against his own. When he lifted his gaze to survey the steps ahead, the back of his skull met the crown of the dead man's through the plastic bag—birthdays and deathdays pressed tight, two halves of a single coin.

Mission carried them both, that load meant for two. He took the stairs a pair at a time, a brutal pace, up toward the farm of his youth.

The coroner's office was on the farm's lower level, tucked away at the end of those dark and damp halls that wound their way beneath the roots. The ceiling was low in that half level. Pipes hung visible from above and rattled angrily as pumps kicked on and moved nutrients to distant and thirsty roots. Water dripped from dozens of small leaks into buckets and pots. A recently emptied pot banged metallic with each strike. Another overflowed. The floors were slick, the walls damp like sweaty skin.

Inside her office, the boys lifted the body onto a slab of dented metal, and the coroner signed Mission's work log. She tipped them for the speedy delivery, and when Cam saw the extra chits, his grumpiness over the pace dissolved. Back in the hallway, he bid Mission good day and splashed toward the exit to find some vice to pair with the bonus.

Mission watched him go, feeling much more than a year older than his friend. Cam hadn't been told of the evening's plans, the midnight rendezvous of porters. This seemed to set them apart, his being privy to adult and dangerous things. It made him envy Cam for what the boy didn't know.

Not wanting to arrive at the farms deadheading and have his father lecture him on laziness, Mission stopped by the maintenance room to see if anything needed carrying up. Winters was on duty, a dark man with a white beard and a knack with pumps. He regarded Mission suspiciously and claimed he hadn't the budget for portering. Mission explained he was going up anyway and that he was glad to take anything.

"In that case," Winters said. He hoisted a monstrous water pump onto his workbench.

"Just the thing," Mission told him, smiling.

Winters narrowed his eyes as if Mission had worked a bolt loose.

The pump wouldn't fit inside his porter's pack, but the haul straps on the outside of the pack looped nicely across the jutting pipes and sharp fittings. Winters helped him get his arms through the straps and the pump secured to his back. He thanked the old man, which drew another worried frown, and set off and up the half level. Back at the stairwell, the odor of mildew from the wet halls faded, replaced by the smell of loam and freshly tilled soil, scents of home that yanked Mission back in time.

The landing on nineteen was crowded as a jam of people attempted to squeeze inside the farms for the day's food. Standing apart from them was a mother in farmer green cradling a wailing child. She had the stains on her knees of a picker and the agitated look of one sent out of the grow plots to soothe her noisy brood. As Mission crowded past, he heard between the baby's cries the words of a familiar nursery rhyme. The mother rocked the child frightfully close to the railing, the infant's eyes wide with what looked to Mission like unadulterated fear.

He worked his way through the crowd, and the cries from the infant receded amid the general din. It occurred to Mission how few kids he saw anymore. It wasn't like when he was young. There had been an explosion of newborns after the violence the last generation had wrought, but now it was just the trickle of natural deaths and the handful of lottery winners. It meant fewer babies crying and fewer parents rejoicing.

With much cajoling and claiming the passage of a porter, he eventually made it through the doors and into the main hall. Using his 'chief, Mission wiped the sweat from his lips. He'd forgotten to top up his canteen a level below, and his mouth was dry. The reasons for pushing so swift a pace felt silly now. It was as if his looming birthday were some deadline to beat, and so the sooner he visited and got away the better. But now in the wash of sights and sounds from his childhood, his dark and angry thoughts melted. It was home, and Mission hated how good it felt to be there.

There were a few hellos and waves as he worked his way toward the gates. Some porters he knew were loading sacks of fruits and vegetables to haul up to the cafeteria. He saw his aunt working one of the vending stalls outside the security gate. After giving up chipping, she now performed the questionably legal act of vending, something she'd never shadowed for. Mission did his best not to catch her eye; he didn't want to get sucked into a lecture or have his hair mussed and his 'chief straightened.

Beyond the stalls, a handful of younger kids clustered in the far corner where it was dark, probably dealing seeds, not looking nearly as inconspicuous as they likely thought. The entire scene in the entrance hall was one of a second bazaar, of farmers selling direct, of people crowding in from distant levels to get food they feared would never make it to their shops and stores. It was fear begetting fear, crowds becoming throngs, and it was easy to see how mobs were next.

Working the main security gate was Frankie, a tall and skinny kid Mission had grown up with. Mission wiped his forehead with the front of his undershirt, which was already cool and damp with sweat. "Hey, Frankie," he called out.

"Mission." A nod and a smile. No hard feelings from another kid who'd jumped shadows long ago. Frankie's father worked in security, down in IT. Frankie had wanted to become a farmer, which Mission never understood. Their teacher, Mrs. Crowe, had been delighted and had encouraged Frankie to follow his dreams. And now Mission found it ironic that Frankie had ended up working security for the farms. It was as if he couldn't escape what he'd been born to do.

Mission smiled and nodded at Frankie's hair. "Did someone splash you with grow quick?"

Frankie tugged on his locks, which were nearly down to his shoulders. "I know, right? My mother threatens to come up here and knife it in my sleep."

"Tell her I'll hold you down while she does it," Mission said, laughing. "Buzz me through?"

There was a wider gate to the side for wheelbarrows and trolleys. Mission didn't feel like squeezing through the turnstiles with the massive pump strapped to his back. Frankie hit a button, and the gate buzzed. Mission pushed his way through.

"Whatcha haulin'?" Frankie asked.

"Water pump from Winters. How've you been?"

Frankie scanned the crowds beyond the gate. "Hold on a sec," he said, looking for someone. Two farmers swiped their work badges and marched through the turnstiles, jabbering away. Sweat dripped from Mission's nose. Frankie waved over someone in green and asked if they could cover for him while he went to the bathroom.

"C'mon," Frankie told Mission. "Walk me."

The two old friends headed down the main hall toward the bright aura of distant grow lights. The smells were intoxicating and familiar. Mission wondered what those same smells meant to Frankie, who had grown up six levels down near the fetid stink of the water plant. Perhaps this reeked to him the way the plant did to Mission. Perhaps the water plant brought back fond memories, instead.

"Things are going nuts around here," Frankie whispered once they were away from the gates.

Mission nodded. "Yeah, I saw a few more stalls had sprouted up. More of them every day, huh?"

Frankie held Mission's arm and slowed their pace so they'd have more time to talk. There was the smell of fresh bread from one of the offices. It was too far from the bakery for warm bread, but such was the new way of things. Probably ground the flour somewhere deep in the farms.

"You've seen what they're doing up in the cafe, right?" Frankie asked.

"I took a load up that way a few weeks ago," Mission said. He tucked his thumbs under his shoulder straps and wiggled the heavy pump higher onto his hips. "I saw they were building something by the wallscreens. Didn't see what."

"They're starting sprouts up there," Frankie said. "Corn, too, supposedly." They stopped by the public restrooms. The sound of a loud flush on the other side of the wall flicked a switch inside Mission's bladder and made him need to go.

"I guess that'll mean fewer runs for us between here and there," Mission said, thinking like a porter. He tapped the wall with the toe of his boot. "Roker'll be pissed when he hears."

Frankie bit his lip and narrowed his eyes. "Yeah, but wasn't Roker the one who started growin' his own beans down in Dispatch?"

Mission wiggled his shoulders. His arms were going numb. He wasn't used to standing still with a load—he was used to moving. "That's different," he argued. He tried to remember why it was different. "That's for climbing food."

Frankie shook his head. "Yeah, but ain't that hypercritical of him?"

"You mean hypocritical?"

"Whatever, man. All I'm saying is everyone has an excuse. We're doing it because they're doing it and someone else started it. So what if we're doing it a little more than they are? That's the attitude, man. But then we get in a twist when the next group does it a little more. It's like a ratchet, the way these things work."

Mission glanced down the hall toward the glow of distant lights. "I dunno," he said. "The mayor seems to be letting things slide lately."

Frankie laughed. "You really think the mayor's in charge? The mayor's scared, man. Scared and *old*." Frankie glanced back down the hall to make sure nobody was coming. The nervousness and paranoia had been in him since his youth. It'd been amusing when he was younger; now it was sad and a little worrisome. "You remember when we talked about being in charge one day?" Frankie asked. "How things would be different?"

"It doesn't work like that," Mission said. "By the time we're in charge, we'll be old like them and won't care anymore. And then *our* kids can hate us for pulling the same crap."

Frankie laughed, and the tension in his wiry frame seemed to subside. "I bet you're right."

"Yeah, well, I need to go before my arms fall off." He shrugged the pump higher up his back.

Frankie slapped his shoulder. "Yeah. Good seeing you, man."

"Same." Mission nodded and turned to go.

"Oh, hey, Mish."

He stopped and looked back.

"You gonna see the Crow anytime soon?"

"I'll pass that way tomorrow," he said, assuming he'd live through the night.

Frankie smiled. "Tell her I said hey, wouldja?"

"I will," Mission promised.

One more name to add to the list. If only he could charge his friends for all the messages he ran for them, he'd have way more than the three-hundred eighty-four chits already saved up. Half a chit for every hello he passed to the Crow, and he'd have his own apartment by now. He wouldn't need to stay in the waystations. He could ask Jenine to marry him. But messages from friends weighed far less than dark thoughts, so Mission didn't mind them taking up space. They crowded out the other. And Lord knew, Mission hauled his fair share of the heavier kind.

·3·

I t would've made more sense and been kinder on Mission's back to drop off the pump before visiting his father, but the whole point of hauling it up was so his old man would see him with the load. And so he headed into the planting halls and toward the same growing station his grandfather had worked and supposedly his great-grandfather, too. Past the beans and the blueberry vines, beyond the squash and the lurking potatoes. In a spot of corn that looked ready for harvest, he found his old man on his hands and knees looking how Mission would always remember him. With a small spade working the soil, his hands picked at weeds like a habit, the way a girl might curl her fingers in her hair over and over without even knowing she was doing it.

"Father."

His old man turned his head to the side, sweat glistening on his brow under the heat of the grow lights. There was a flash of a smile before it melted. Mission's half-brother Riley appeared behind a back row of corn, a little twelve-year-old mimic of his dad, hands covered in dirt. He was quicker to call out a greeting, shouting "Mission!" as he hurried to his feet.

"The corn looks good," Mission said. He rested a hand on the railing, the weight of the pump settling against his back, and reached out to bend a leaf with his thumb. Moist. The ears were a few weeks from harvest, and the smell took him right back. He saw a midge running up the stalk and killed the parasite with a deft pinch.

"Wadja bring me?" his little brother squealed.

Mission laughed and tussled his brother's dark hair, a gift from the boy's mother. "Sorry, bro. They loaded me down this time." He turned slightly so Riley could see, but also for his father. His brother stepped onto the lowest rail and leaned over for a better look.

"Why dontcha set that down for a while?" his father asked. He slapped his hands together to keep the precious dirt on the proper side of the fence, then reached out and shook Mission's hand. "You're looking good."

"You too, Dad." Mission would've thrust his chest out and stood taller if it didn't mean toppling back on his rear from the pump. "So what's this I hear about the cafe starting in their own sprouts?"

His father grumbled and shook his head. "Corn, too, from what I hear. More goddamn up-sourcing." He jabbed a finger at Mission's chest. "This affects you lads, you know."

His father meant the porters, and there was a tone of having told him so. There was always that tone. Riley tugged on Mission's coveralls and asked to hold his porter knife. Mission slid the blade from its sheath and handed it over while he studied his father, a heavy silence brewing. His dad looked older. His skin was the color of oiled wood, an unhealthy darkness from working too long under the grow lights. It was called a "tan," and you could spot a farmer two landings away because of it, could pick them out by their skin like burnt toast.

Mission could feel the intense heat radiating from the bulbs overhead, and the anger he felt when he was away from home melted into a hollow sadness. The spot of air his mother had left empty could be felt. It was a reminder to Mission of what his being born had cost. More was the pity that he felt for his old man with his damaged skin and dark spots on his nose from years of abuse. These were the signs of all those in green who toiled among the dead. And this was where his father would have Mission work as well, if it were up to him.

While his father studied him and Riley played with the knife, Mission flashed back to his first solid memory as a boy. Wielding a small spade that had in those days seemed to him a giant shovel, he had been playing between the rows of corn, turning over scoops of soil, mimicking his father, when without warning his old man had grabbed his wrist.

"Don't dig there," his father had said with an edge to his voice. This was back before Mission had witnessed his first funeral, before he had seen for himself what went beneath the seeds. After that day, he learned to spot the mounds where the soil was dark from being disturbed. He learned to study the way those same mounds gradually sank and leveled out as the worms carried off what lay beneath.

"They've got you doing the heavy lifting, I see," his father said, breaking the quiet. He assumed the load Mission had begged for was instead assigned by Dispatch. Mission didn't correct him.

"They let us carry what we can handle," he said. "The older porters get mail delivery. We each haul what we can."

"I remember when I first stepped out of the shadows," his dad said. He squinted and wiped his brow, nodded down the line.

"Got stuck with potatoes while my caster went back to plucking blueberries. Two for the basket and one for him."

Not this again. Mission watched as Riley tested the tip of the knife with the pad of his finger. He reached to take back the blade, but his brother twisted away from him.

"The older porters get mail duty because they *can* get mail duty," his father explained.

"You don't know what you're talking about," Mission said. The sadness was gone, the anger back. "The old ports have bad knees is why we get the loads. Besides, my bonus pay is judged by the pound and the time I make, so I don't mind."

"Oh, yes." His father waved at Mission's feet. "They pay you in bonuses and you pay them with your knees."

Mission could feel his cheeks tighten, could sense the burn of the whelp around his neck.

"All I'm saying, son, is that the older you get and the more seniority, you'll earn your own choice of rows to hoe. That's all. I want you to watch out for yourself."

"I'm watching out for myself, Dad." He nearly added: *It isn't like I have anyone else*.

Riley climbed up, sat on the top rail, and flashed his teeth at his own reflection in the knife. The kid already had that band of spots across his nose, those freckles, the start of a tan. Damaged flesh from damaged flesh, father like son. And Mission could easily picture Riley years hence on the other side of that rail, could see his half-brother all grown up with a kid of his own, and it made Mission thankful that he'd wormed his way out of the farms and into a job he didn't take home every night beneath his fingernails.

"Are you joining us for lunch?" his father asked, sensing perhaps that he was pushing Mission away. A change in subjects was as near to an apology as the old man dared.

"If you don't mind," Mission said. He felt a twinge of guilt that his father expected to feed him, but he appreciated not having to ask. "I'll have to run afterward, though. I've got a . . . delivery tonight."

His father frowned. "You'll have time to see Allie though, right? She's forever asking about you. The boys here are lined up to marry that girl if you keep her waiting."

Mission wiped his face to hide his expression. Allie was a great friend—his first and briefest romance—but to marry her would be to marry the farms, to return home, to live among the dead. "Probably not this time," he said. And he felt bad for admitting it.

"Okay. Well, go drop that off. Don't squander your bonus sitting here jawing with us." The disappointment in the old man's voice was hotter than the lights and not so easy to shade. "We'll see you in the feeding hall in half an hour?" He reached out, took his son's hand one more time, and gave it a squeeze. "It's good to see you, Son."

"Same." Mission shook his father's hand, then clapped his palms together over the grow pit to knock loose any dirt. Riley reluctantly gave the knife back, and Mission slipped it into its sheath. He fastened the clasp around the handle, thinking on how he might need it that night. He pondered for a moment if he should warn his father, thought of telling him and Riley both to stay inside until morning, to not dare go out.

But he held his tongue, patted his brother on the shoulder, and made his way to the pump room. As he walked through rows of planters and pickers, he thought about farmers selling their own vegetables in makeshift stalls. He thought about the cafe growing its own sprouts. He thought of the plans recently discovered to move something heavy from one landing to another without involving the porters.

Everyone was trying to do it all in case the violence returned. Mission could feel it brewing, the suspicion and the distrust, the walls being built. Everyone was trying to get a little less reliant on the others, preparing for the inevitable, hunkering down.

He loosened the straps on his pack as he approached the pump room, and a dangerous thought occurred to him, a revelation: Everyone was trying to get to where they didn't *need* one another. And how exactly was that supposed to help them all get along?

·4·

After the best meal he'd had in ages—as fresh as it was free—Mission hurried down four flights toward Sanitation to see Jenine. He felt light as a feather downbound and with the load off. With just his empty porter's pack on his back, his canteen jouncing on one hip, his knife on the other, he skipped down the steps side-style with one hand on the rail. At times like these, descending after a long slog up, it felt as though he could leap over the rail and float unharmed to Mechanical like a mote of dust. He apologized to those he overtook, saying "porter, ma'am" and "porter, sir" by the book, even though he wasn't carrying anything official.

Weightless as a bird, with his heart thrumming like one was trapped in his ribcage, it occurred to him that maybe it wasn't the descent that had him feeling giddy. Everyone expected him to grow up a farmer, to settle down with the girl who loved him, but Mission wanted the opposite of what was easily attainable. He wondered if this was a punishment of sorts, a slow strangulation, his thirst for distant things. Did he love the chase? Or was it that staying on the move made it more difficult for the past to catch up to him?

He arrived at Sanitation, a rumble of footfalls on steel treads, and pushed through doors in need of oil. Sanitation was one of the levels laid out in a spiral; a single hallway coiled its way from the landing and did three circuits before dead ending into the waste plant. Fresh water emerged near the landing and was piped out to the rest of the Up Top, while gray water and black water—euphemisms both—were pumped into the waste room. The gray came from showers, sinks, and drains, the black from toilets.

Such were the romantic and decidedly un-sexy conversations Mission had with the girl of his dreams that he could name the plant's every phase of operation as he wound his way toward the waste room. If needed, he could also bore a porter to tears with rumors of who had said what about whom throughout the plant. This was the mark of deep infatuation, he thought: the desire to watch a woman talk just to see her lips move, to be around her.

The noise along the curving hallway grew louder the deeper he went. It started out as a background hum near the control rooms and offices, and just when he'd gotten used to this residual noise, another layer piled on top, more machines macerating, filtering, straining, and pumping. Mission never appreciated how loud the combined buzzing was until he left the plant with his hearing rattled and his throat sore from yelling over it all.

Inside the waste room, he spotted familiar faces all around the processing vats. Knowing who he was looking for, one of the workers pointed down the long row of low steel cylinders that held the gray and black water. Jenine was on top of one of the cylinders, which was almost as big around as his dad's apartment and crisscrossed with pipes and valves. Crouched down, she worked a series of large valves while an older woman filled a glass vial with murky fluid and held it up to the light. Mission waited patiently. This was where the water eventually came from that his father was always cursing. He remembered his old man sitting around the dinner table, shaking his fist at the floor, grumbling about the supply of water, how it was more than he needed for his crops one day, never enough the next.

Jenine eventually felt his presence. She turned, smiled, and lifted a finger, asking him to wait a moment, then finished opening and closing the valves. The woman testing the waste water glanced up at the two of them, frowned at Mission, and carefully dispensed a dark dye into the tube before shaking it, a thumb unhygienically used to cork the end. These were dark arts, Mission thought, whatever they did to make shower water and urine safe to drink. Dark and noisy arts. But at least he had grown used to the smell, which wasn't the foulness one would expect but rather something chemical, something caustic.

Jenine yelled to her supervisor that she was taking her break, wiped her palms on the seat of her pants, and hopped down. She led Mission away from the rows and rows of containers before digging the foam inserts out of her ears.

"Hey, Mish!" she yelled, as she pulled him into the hallway. She clasped his neck and kissed him on the cheek. By the time he thought to hug her back or return the gesture, it was already over, leaving him scrambling awkwardly at the air and feeling a fool.

She led him down two doors to the break room, which stank of microwaved soup and sweaty coveralls. It smelled almost exactly like the break room in Dispatch, fifty levels down, in fact. Mission wondered if every break room smelled just like this.

Jenine grabbed a dented metal cup from a pile of them by the sink and filled it with water. "Whadja bring me?" she asked, glancing at his shoulder.

Mission shook his head and turned to show her his empty pack. "I'm sorry," he said, feeling like an ass.

She waved her hand and took a long pull on the tin cup. "It's fine." She refilled the cup from the sink, and Mission noticed that she waited for the faucet to stop dripping into the vessel, even tapped it twice with her fist to get the last drop, before pulling it away. Every profession had its quirks and habits, he supposed. Like how a porter never passed a landing without checking for a signal 'chief, nor missed a rumor whispered on the stairs.

"Sorry if I made it sound like it's your duty to shower me with gifts." She winked at him, and Mission laughed.

"Don't be sorry," he said. "I like bringing you stuff. I was just weighed down with a tandem haul this time." He swung his arms and twisted at the waist to stretch his spine. "They've been pouring it on us. But this is what I've been told to expect our first year."

"Tell me about it." Jenine leaned back against the counter and waved Mission toward the jumbled pile of cups. "I thought shadowing was bad, but first year is even worse."

He accepted her offer and filled a cup with water. He reminded himself to top up his thermos before he left as well.

"It's almost enough to make you miss school, isn't it?" she asked.

Mission laughed. "Oh, hell yeah it is."

"Here's to better days." She held her cup up.

Mission tinked his against hers, careful not to splash any water. "To better days."

They watched each other over the lips of their cups while they drank. And in that breathless pause, in the time it took to swallow once, twice, three times, Mission felt an incredible rush of happiness that just as quickly plummeted away. It was like a memory of something that had not yet happened, a vivid image of him and Jenine sitting at a small table in a small apartment, and then a sense of the space between them brought on by their occupations. In this imaginary future, he would find himself leaving for another week of runs before he got his next day off. And so the same dread he felt right then in that break room, the desire to maximize their time together, to sip rather than gulp, would surely haunt him in a future he could only dream about. He swallowed and peered into his cup, searching for the courage to tell her how he felt.

"Speaking of better days," Jenine said, "have you been by the Nest lately?"

Mission shook his head. He finished his water with another long pull and filled it halfway back up. "I will tomorrow." He turned and studied his friend and had a sudden sense of how grown up they had become, standing around like that, both with jobs, sipping water from dented cups, swapping memories of the long ago. "You?"

She nodded. "I was up last weekend. A few of us are trying to go more regularly, help with the kids, though there aren't as many of them around as there used to be."

"A few of you? Did Rodny go?"

He braced himself for her reply. An old rumor had spread that the two of them had been spending time together, back before Rodny was swallowed up by his work. Jenine was going to tell him that yes, she and Rodny were in love, had made it official, had registered with the Pact. She was going to tell him and break his heart—

"I haven't seen Rod in a while. I was going to ask you. Whatever they have him doing in IT, they don't seem to let him out much."

Mission shrugged and feigned indifference. In fact, he had grown concerned. The last two times he'd been through the thirties and stopped to see his friend, he'd been told Rodny was "unavailable." Even when Mission insisted he didn't mind waiting, they'd told him it wouldn't happen. Mission worried his old friend was becoming a recluse or a workaholic, one more piece of his childhood wrested away. He used to laugh when Rodny boasted he'd be Mayor or a department head one day. It didn't seem so funny anymore.

"I have to get back," Jenine said. "I only get a ten." She grabbed a small towel from a hanger over the sink and rubbed the cup inside and out. She set it back on the pile and held her hand out for Mission's. "You got another delivery today, or are you done?"

"I'm done." He finished his water and let her have the cup. "I'm crashing in the waystation on nineteen. I might do a run up-top before heading down to see the Crow tomorrow."

"So what're you doing tonight?" She waved her consent as Mission held up his thermos questioningly. "You wanna hang out? Me and some friends are going up to twenty-three to drop paint bombs."

"I can't tonight." His metal thermos sang as it was filled, and he felt doubly bad for not bringing her anything. "I've got this thing later."

"What thing? I thought you were gonna sack out."

"I meant that I have to get up early. And haven't you gotten a little old for paint bombs?"

Jenine smiled. "There's this place on twenty-three where if you release at just the right spot, the bomb goes almost a hundred levels down before splatting at one-twenty-two."

Mission shifted his weight to his other foot. "Yeah, I've seen it." He wanted to tell her that he walked through that spot on one-twenty-two all the time, that people he knew down there complained, that Sharen, another porter, had nearly been hit by a paint bomb dropped from the Mids a few weeks ago. Instead, he told Jenine about the time something had whistled by his head in the dead of night as he worked his way through the eighties. "Maybe it's not such a good idea," he told her.

Jenine's smile melted. She didn't say anything, didn't have to—the silence was enough. It was as if she were beginning to understand something even better than Mission did: he was no longer just of the Up Top. He was a child of the entire silo, now. It meant more than being a target everywhere he went. It meant having no one to conspire with anymore, no one to pick out targets with in whispers.

"Well, you've gotta get up early tomorrow, anyway."

"Yeah." He brushed his hair off his forehead. All the barbers he passed in a typical week, never enough time to stop. He would look like Frankie soon enough. "Hey, it was good seeing you."

"Same. For sure. Take care of yourself, Mish. Watch your steps."

Mission smiled. And this time, when she leaned in to touch his neck and kiss his cheek, he was ready to reciprocate. "You know I will," he said, kissing her lightly on the cheek. "You watch your steps as well."

·5·

L ater that night, Mission could still feel the soft touch of her hand on his neck and the press of her lips to his cheek. In the quiet and deathly darkness of the silo's nighttime, he could hear Jenine whispering for him to be safe.

The lights had been dimmed so man and silo might sleep. It was those wee hours when children were long hushed with sing-song lullabies and only those with trouble in mind crept about. Mission held very still in that darkness and waited. He thought on love and other forbidden things. And somewhere in the dark, there came the chirp of rope wound tight and sliding against metal, the bird-like sound fibers made as they gripped steel and strained under some great burden.

A gang of porters huddled with him on the stairway. Mission pressed his cheek against the silo's untrembling inner post, the cool steel touching him where Jenine's lips had. He lost himself in his thoughts, controlling his breathing like he'd been shadowed how. And he listened for the rope. He knew well the sounds they made, could feel the burn on his neck, that raised weal healed over by the years, a mark glanced at by others but rarely mentioned aloud. And again in that thick gray of the dim-time there came a chirp like some caged bird flexing its beak.

He waited for the signal. He thought on rope, his own life, and secret love—all these forbidden things. There was a book in Dispatch down on seventy-four that kept accounts. In the main waystation for all the porters, a massive ledger fashioned out of a fortune in paper was kept under lock and key. On this year's wage of pulp was a careful tally of certain types of deliveries, handwritten so the information couldn't slip off into wires. Only a handful of porters knew for certain it existed—to the rest the book was legend.

Mission had heard that they kept track of certain kinds of pipe in this ledger, but he didn't know why. Brass, too, and various types of fluids coming out of Chemical. Any of these or too much rope, and you were put on the watching list. Porters were the lords of rumor. They knew where everything went. And their whisperings gathered like condensation in Dispatch Main where they were written down.

Mission listened to the rope creak and sing in the darkness. He knew what it felt like to have a length of it cinched tightly around his neck. And it seemed strange to him—it seemed wrong—that if you ordered enough to hang yourself, nobody cared. Enough to span a few levels, and eyebrows were raised.

He adjusted his handkerchief and thought on this in the dim-time. A man may take his own life, he supposed, as long as he didn't take another's job.

"Ready yourself," came the whisper from above.

Mission tightened the grip on his knife and concentrated on the task at hand. His eyes strained to see in the wan light. The steady breathing of his neighbors was occasionally heard. They would be squeezing their own knives or their empty and angry fists.

The knives came with the job—they were as much a part of porting as the inverted hearts that grew on practiced calves. A porter's knife for slicing open delivered goods, for cutting fruit to eat on the climb, and for keeping peace as its owner strayed from all the heights and depths, taking the silo's dangers two at a time. It was said that a porter's knife shadowed for a thousand jobs, that its caster was its owner, its home a good sheath. Here waited but another job for Mission's gleaming shadow. With the flick of a wrist, it would quiet the neck of that singing bird. It would part a rope that groaned under a darkened and illicit strain.

Up the stairwell two full turns, on a dim landing, a group of farmers argued in soft voices as they handled the other end of that rope, as they performed a porter's job in the dark of night that they might save a hundred chits or two. Beyond the rail across from Mission, a black shape slid past. The rope was invisible in the inky void. He would have to lean out and grope for the chirping bird's neck. He felt a ring of heat by his collar, and the hilt of his blade felt unsure in his sweating palm.

"Not yet," Morgan whispered, and Mission felt his old caster's hand on his shoulder, holding him back, still treating him like a shadow even now. Mission cleared his mind. Another soft chirp, the sound of line taking the strain of a heavy generator, and a dense patch of gray drifted through the black. The men above shouted in whispers as they handled the load, as they did in green the work of men in blue.

While the patch of gray inched past, Mission thought of the night's danger and marveled at the fear in his heart. He possessed a sudden care for a life he had once labored to end, a life that never should've been. He thought of his mother and wondered what she was like, beyond her disobedience. That was all he knew of her. He knew the implant in her hip had failed, as one in ten thousand might. And instead of reporting the malfunction—and the pregnancy—she had hid him in loose clothes until it was past the time the Pact allowed a child to be treated as a cyst.

"Ready yourself," Morgan hissed.

The gray mass of the generator crept down and out of sight. Mission clutched his knife and thought of how he should've been cut out of her and discarded. But past a certain date, and one life was traded for another. Such was the Pact. Born behind bars, Mission had been allowed free while his mother had been sent outside. In the middle of the night, she must've watched as they cleaned the blood from his wailing flesh. By the morning, she was cleaning for them all.

"Now," Morgan commanded, and Mission startled. Soft and well-worn boots squeaked on the stairs above, the sounds of men lurching into action. Mission concentrated on his part. He pressed himself against the curved rail and reached out into the space beyond. His palm found rope as stiff as steel, and he thought of the great depths below him, how long the fall. He remembered less dangerous games with paint bombs and paper parachutes as he pressed his blade to the taut line.

There was a pop like sinew snapping, the first of the braids parting with just a touch of his sharp blade.

Mission had but a moment to think of those on the landing below, the accomplices waiting two levels down. Another pop, and the wounded bird sang at a different pitch. Men were storming up the staircase. Mission longed to join them. With the barest of sawing motions, the rope parted the rest of the way and let out a twangy cry. Mission thought he heard the heavy generator whistle as it picked up speed. There was a ferocious crash a moment later, men screaming in alarm down below, but those screams could've been coming from anywhere. The fighting had broken out above.

With one hand on the rail and another strangling his knife, Mission took the stairs three at a time. He rushed to join the melee above, this midnight lesson on breaking the Pact, on doing another's job.

Grunts and groans and slapping thuds spilled from the landing, and Mission threw himself into the scuffle, thinking not where wars come from but only on this one battle. His feet tangled briefly in forbidden rope, all those shorter strands twisted and woven into something bigger, a line long enough to tangle a thousand souls.

• Silo 1 •

A second shift.

"The mind is its own place, and in itself
Can make a heaven of hell, a hell of heaven."

- John Milton

·6·

The wheelchair squeaked as its wheels went 'round and 'round. With each revolution there was a sharp peal of complaint followed by a circuit of deathly silence. Donald lost himself in this rhythmic sound. He began to anticipate each chirp, like a lonely bird crying for its mate. Chirp and silence. Chirp and silence. As he was pushed along, his breath puffed out into the air, the room harboring the same deep chill as his bones.

There were rows and rows of pods stretched out to either side. Names glowed orange on tiny screens. Made-up names. Phony names designed to sever the past from the now. Donald watched them slide by as they pushed him toward the exit. His head felt heavy, his neck inadequate for propping up his skull, the weight of remembrance replacing the wisps of dreams that coiled away and vanished like vaporous smoke.

The men in the pale blue coveralls guided him through the door and into the hallway, and Donald seemed to float along like a ghost, like a man disturbed from his grave. He was steered into a familiar room with a familiar table. Boots kicked here—he remembered from a dream. In one dream, he was the one holding the boots still, bones like a bird's struggling beneath his grip, and he was the enemy. In another dream it was *his* boots doing the kicking. He could see them at the ends of his own legs while ice burned in his veins.

The wheelchair shimmied as they removed his bare feet from the footrests. He asked how long it'd been, how long he'd been asleep.

"Seventy years," someone said. He did the math. A hundred and twenty since orientation. No wonder the wheelchair felt unsteady—it was older than he was. Its screws had worked loose over the long decades that Donald had been asleep.

They helped him stand. His feet were still numb from his hibernation, the cold fading to painful tingles. A noisy curtain was drawn. They asked him to urinate in a cup, which came as glorious relief. The sample was the color of charcoal, dead machines flushed from his system. The paper gown wasn't enough to warm him, even though he knew the cold was in his flesh, not in the room. They gave him more of the bitter drink.

"How long before his head is clear?" someone asked.

"A day," the doctor said. "Tomorrow at the earliest."

They had him sit while they took his blood. A man in white coveralls with hair just as stark stood in the doorway, frowning. "Save your strength," the man said. He nodded to the doctor to continue his work and disappeared before Donald could place him in his faltering memory. He felt dizzy and watched as his blood, blue from the cold, was taken from him.

• • • •

They rode a familiar elevator. The men around him talked, but their voices were drones behind a slowly parting fog. Donald felt as though he had been drugged, but he remembered that he had stopped taking their pills. He reached for his bottom lip, finger and mouth both tingling, and felt for an ulcer, that little pocket where he kept his pills unswallowed.

But the ulcer wasn't there. It would've healed in his sleep decades ago. The lift dinged, the doors parted, and Donald felt more of that dreamtime fade.

They pushed him down another hall, scuff marks on the walls the height of the wheels, black arcs where rubber had once met the paint. His eyes roamed the walls, the ceiling, the tiles, all bearing centuries of wear. Like the wheelchair, these halls never slept. Yesterday, they were almost new. Now they were heaped with abuse, a jarring eyeblink of decrepitude, a sudden crumbling into ruin. Donald remembered designing halls just like these. He remembered thinking they were making something to last for ages. The truth was there all along. The truth was in the design, staring back at him, too insane to be taken seriously.

The wheelchair slowed.

"The next one," a voice behind him said, a gruff voice, an exhausted and familiar voice. Donald was pushed past one closed door to another. One of the orderlies bustled around the wheelchair, a ring of keys jangling from his hip. A key was selected and slotted into the knob with a series of neat clicks. Hinges cried out as the door was pushed inward. The lights inside were turned on.

It was a room like a cell, musky with the scent of disuse. There was a narrow double bunk in the corner, a side table, a dresser, a bathroom. The light overhead flickered before it came on, like a tingling hand that needed a moment before forming a fist.

"Why am I here?" Donald asked, his voice cracking.

"This will be your room," the orderly said, putting away his keys. His young eyes darted up to the man steering the wheelchair as if unsure of the rightness of his answer. Another young man in pale blue hurried around and removed Donald's feet from the stirrups and placed them on carpet worn flat by the years.

Donald's last memory was of being chased by snarling dogs with leathery wings, chased up a mountain of bones. But that was a dream. What was his last *real* memory? It was the one of being put to sleep for good. He remembered a needle. He remembered dying. That felt real.

"I mean—" Donald swallowed painfully. "Why am I . . . *awake?*"

He almost said alive. The two orderlies exchanged glances as they helped him from the chair to the lower bunk. The wheelchair squeaked once as it was pushed back into the hallway. The man guiding it paused, his broad shoulders making the doorway appear small.

One of the orderlies held Donald's wrist—two fingers pressing lightly on ice-blue veins, lips silently counting. The other orderly dropped two pills into a plastic cup and fumbled with the cap on a bottle of water.

"That won't be necessary," the silhouette in the doorway said.

The orderly with the pills glanced over his shoulder, and Donald remembered that these weren't orderlies at all. They were the other kind of doctors. Doctors of the body, not of the mind.

"I remember," Donald muttered. He pictured himself inside a straw plunged deep into the dirt. There were other straws around him, concrete tombs lined with pipe and wire, things that he could draw, that he had designed.

The man in the doorway stepped inside the small room, and some of the air was displaced. "Good," he said, in that familiar voice, that old voice. The room shrank further. It became more difficult to breathe.

"You're the Thaw—" Donald whispered.

The old man with the white hair waved a hand at the two doctors. "Give us a moment," he said. The one with a grip on Donald's wrist finished his counting and nodded to the other. Unswallowed pills rattled in a paper cup as they were put away.

"I remember everything," Donald said, though he suspected this wasn't quite true. "You're the Thaw Man."

A smile was flashed, as white as his hair, wrinkles forming around his lips and eyes. The chair in the hallway squeaked as it was pushed away, off to retrieve someone else, never sleeping. The door clicked shut. Donald thought he heard a lock engage, but his teeth still chattered occasionally, and his ears were full of lead.

"Thurman," the man said, correcting him. "But I don't go by that anymore. Just as you don't go by Donald."

"But I remember," Donald said. More came back to him. He remembered his office, the one upstairs and some other office far away, some place where it still rained and the grass grew. This man had been a Senator. But of what? Donald remembered drawing this place.

"And that's a mystery we need to solve." The senator of nothing tilted his head. "For now, it's good that you do. We *need* you to remember."

Thurman leaned against the metal dresser. He looked as though he hadn't slept in days. His hair was unkempt, not quite how Donald remembered it. There were dark circles beneath his sad eyes. He seemed much . . . older, somehow.

Donald peered down at his own palms, the springs in the bed making the room feel as though it were swaying. He flashed again to the horrible sight of a man remembering his own name and wanting to be free.

"Who am I?" he asked. He had felt so certain a moment before. Had he swallowed those pills? No, he remembered them rattling back into that orderly's coat. That *doctor's* coat. This was just the waking confusion. It would pass, he told himself. This was the groggy morning after a century of vivid dreams.

"Who do you think you are?" the Thaw Man asked. He produced a folded piece of paper and waited for an answer. Recollections came back and then receded like a sea swelling in and out against a pier.

"My name is Donald Keene."

"So you do remember. And you know who I am."

Donald nodded.

"Good." The Thaw Man turned and placed the folded piece of paper on the dresser. He arranged it on its bent legs so it tented upward, toward the ceiling. "We need you to remember everything," he said. "Study this report when the fog clears, see if it jars anything loose. Once your stomach is settled, I'll have a proper meal brought down."

Donald rubbed his temples. The sea drew away from the pier.

"You've been gone for some time," the Thaw Man said. He rapped his knuckles on the door.

Donald wiggled his bare toes against the carpet. The sensation was returning to his feet. The door clicked before swinging open, and the Senator once again blocked the light spilling from the hallway. He became a shadow for a moment.

"Rest, and then we'll get our answers together. There's someone who wants to see you."

The room was sealed tight before Donald could ask what that meant. And somehow, with the door shut and him gone, there was more air to breathe in that small space. Donald took a few deep breaths. He waited for the world to change, for the snarling dogs with the bat-like wings to return, for the mountain of skulls to reappear beneath his scrambling hands and knees, that interminable climb upward to a peak that would not come. But the room was too solid for that. After a long while, he grabbed the frame of the bed and struggled to his feet. He stood there a moment, swaying.

"Get our answers," he repeated aloud. Someone wants to see him.

He shook his head, which made the world spin. As if he had any answers. All he had were questions. He remembered the orderlies who woke him saying something about a silo falling. He couldn't remember which one. Why would they wake him for that?

He moved unsteadily to the door, tried the knob, confirmed what he already knew. He went to the dresser where the piece of paper stood on its remembered folds.

"Get some rest," he said, laughing at the suggestion. As if he could sleep. He felt as though he'd been asleep forever. He picked up the piece of paper and unfolded it.

A report. Donald remembered this. It was a copy of a report. A report about a young man doing horrible things. The room twisted around him as if he stood on some great pivot, the memory of men and women trampled and dying, of giving some awful order, faces peering in at him from a hallway somewhere far in the past. Somewhere like yesterday.

Donald blinked away a curtain of tears and studied the trembling report. Hadn't he written this? He had signed it, he remembered. But that wasn't his name at the bottom. It was his handwriting, but it wasn't his name.

Troy.

Donald's legs went numb. He sought the bed—but collapsed to the floor instead. He kept saying he remembered even as more and more washed over him. Troy and Helen. Helen and Troy. He remembered his wife. He saw her disappearing over a hill, her arm raised to the sky where bombs were falling, his sister and some dark and nameless shadow pulling him back as people spilled like marbles down a slope, spilled and gathered, plunking through a funnel and into some deep hole filled with white mist.

Donald remembered. He remembered all that he had helped do to the world. There was a troubled boy in a silo full of the dead, a shadow among the servers. That boy had brought an end to silo number 12. But Donald— What had he done? There were no numbers to contain all the dead. Their skulls made a pile that reached to the heavens. And the tears that popped against the trembling report, they were tinged a pale blue.

A doctor brought soup and bread a few hours later, plus a tall glass of water. Donald ate hungrily while the man checked his arm. The warm soup felt good. It slid to his center and seemed to radiate its heat outward. He tore at the bread with his teeth and chased it with the water. Somehow these things were going to keep his flesh from collapsing inward. Donald ate with the desperation of so many years of fasting.

"Thank you," he said between bites. "For the food."

The doctor glanced up from checking his blood pressure. He was an older man, heavyset, with great bushy eyebrows and a fine wisp of hair clinging to his scalp like a cloud to a hilltop.

"I'm Donald," he said, introducing himself.

There was a wrinkle of confusion on the old man's brow. His gray eyes strayed toward his clipboard as if either it or his patient couldn't be trusted. The needle on the gauge jumped with Donald's pulse.

"Who're you?" Donald asked.

"I'm Doctor Henson," he finally said, though without confidence.

Donald took a long swig on his water, thankful they'd left it at room temperature. He didn't want anything cold inside him ever again. "Where're you from?"

The doctor removed the cuff from Donald's arm with a loud rip. "Level ten. But I work out of the shift office on sixty-eight." He put his tools back in his bag and made a note on the clipboard.

"No, I mean, where are you *from*. You know . . . before."

Dr. Henson patted Donald's knee and stood. The clipboard went on a hook on the outside of the door. "You might have some dizziness the next few days. Let us know if you experience any trembling, okay?"

Donald nodded. He remembered being given the same advice earlier. Or was that his last shift? Maybe the repetition was for those who had trouble remembering. He wasn't going to be one of those people. Not this time.

A shadow fell into the room. Donald looked up to see the Thaw Man in the doorway. He gripped the meal tray to keep it from sliding off his knees.

The Thaw Man nodded to Dr. Henson, but this was not their names. *Thurman*, Donald told himself. Senator Thurman. He knew this.

"Do you have a moment?" Thurman asked the doctor.

"Of course." Henson grabbed his bag and stepped outside. The door clicked shut, leaving Donald alone with his soup.

He took quiet spoonfuls, trying to make anything of the murmurs on the other side of the door. *Thurman*, he reminded himself again. And not a senator. Senator of what? Those days were gone. Donald had drawn the plans.

The report stood tented on the dresser, returned to its spot.

Donald took a bite of bread and remembered the floors he'd laid out. Those floors were now real. They existed. People lived inside them, raising their children, laughing, having fights, singing in the shower. People lived in the things he'd made, in the holes he'd dug. Those people—and no more.

A few minutes passed before the knob tilted and the door swung inward. The Thaw Man entered the room alone. He pressed the door shut and frowned at Donald. "How're you feeling?"

The spoon clacked against the rim of the bowl. Donald set the utensil down and gripped the tray with both hands to keep them from shaking, to keep them from forming fists.

"You know," Donald hissed, teeth clenched together. "You know what we did."

Thurman showed his palms. "We did what had to be done."

"No. Don't give me that." Donald shook his head. The water in his glass trembled as if something dangerous approached. "The world . . ."

"We saved it."

"That's not true!" Donald's voice cracked. He tried to remember. "There is no world." He recalled the view from the top, from the cafeteria. He remembered the hills a dull brown, the sky full of menacing clouds. "We ended it. We killed everyone."

"They were already dead," Thurman said. "We all were. Everyone dies, son. The only thing that matters is—"

"No." Donald waved the words away as if they were buzzing things that could bite him. "There's no justifying this—" He felt spittle form on his lips, wiped it away with his sleeve. The tray on his lap slid dangerously, and Thurman moved swifter than his years to catch it. He placed what was left of the meal on the bedside table, and up close, Donald could see that he had gotten older. The wrinkles were deeper, the skin hanging from the bones. He wondered how much time Thurman had spent awake while Donald slept.

"I killed a lot of men in the war," Thurman said, looking down at the tray of half-eaten food.

Donald found himself focused on the old man's neck. He interlocked his hands to keep them still. This sudden admission about killing made it seem as if he could read Donald's mind, like this was some kind of a warning for Donald to stay his murderous plans.

Thurman turned to the dresser and picked up the folded report. He opened it, and Donald caught sight of the pale blue dollops, his ice-tinged tears from earlier.

"Some say killing gets easier the longer you're at it," Thurman said. He sounded sad, not threatening. Donald looked down at his own knees and saw that they were bouncing. He forced his heels against the carpet and tried to pin them there.

"For me, it only got worse. There was a man in Iran—"

"The entire goddamn planet," Donald whispered, stressing each word. This was what he said, but all he could think about was his wife. Bombs going off, the plans he'd drawn, Helen pulled down the wrong hill, marbles rolling apart, everything that had ever existed crumbling to ruin. "We killed everyone."

The senator took in a deep breath and held it a moment. "I told you," he said. "They were already dead."

Donald's knees began bouncing again. There was no controlling it. Thurman studied the report, seemed unsure of something. The paper faintly shook, but maybe it was the overhead vent blowing, which also stirred his hair.

"We were outside of Kashmar," Thurman said. "This was toward the end of the war, when we were getting our butts kicked and telling the world we were winning. I had a corporal in my squad, our team medic, a James Hannigan. Young. Always cracking jokes but serious when he needed to be. The kind of guy everyone likes. The hardest kind to lose."

Thurman shook his head. He stared off into the distance. The vent in the ceiling quieted, but the report continued to quiver.

"I killed a lot of men during the war, but only once to really *save* a life. The rest, you never knew what you were doing when you pulled the trigger. Maybe the guy you take out is never gonna find his own target, never hurt a soul. Maybe he's gonna be one of the thousands who drop their rifles and blend in with the civvies, go back to their families, open a kasava stand near the embassy and talk basketball with the troops stationed outside. A good man. You never knew. You're killing these men, and you never knew if you were doing it for a good reason or not."

"How many billions—?" Donald swallowed. He slid to the edge of the bed and reached toward the tray. Thurman knew what he was after and passed the glass of water, half empty. He continued to ignore Donald's complaints.

"Hannigan got hit with shrapnel outside of Kashmar. If we could get him to a medic, it was the kind of wound you survived, the kind you lift your shirt in a bar to show off the scars one day. But he couldn't walk, and it was too hot to send in an airlift. Our squad was hemmed in and would need to fight our way out. I didn't think we could get to a safe LZ in time to save him. But what I knew, because I'd seen it too many damn times before, is that two or three of my men would die trying to get him out. That's what happens when you're lugging a soldier instead of a rifle." Thurman pressed his sleeve to his forehead. "I'd seen it before."

"You left him behind," Donald said, seeing where this was going. He took a sip of water. The surface was agitated.

"No. I killed him." Thurman stared at the foot of the bed. He stared at nothing. "The enemy wouldn't have let him die. Not there, not like that. They would've patched him up so they could catch it on film. They would've stitched up his belly so they could open his throat." He turned to Donald. "I had to make a decision, and I had to make it fast. And the longer I've lived with it, the more I've come to agree with what I did. We lost one man that day. I saved two or three others."

Donald shook his head. "That's not the same as what we— what you—"

"It's precisely the same. Do you remember Safed? What the media called the outbreak?"

Donald remembered Safed. An Israeli town near Nazareth. Near Syria. The deadliest WMD strike of the war. He nodded.

"The rest of the world would've looked just like that. Just like Safed." Thurman snapped his fingers. "Ten billion lights go out all at once. We were already infected, son. It was just a matter of triggering it. Safed was . . . like a beta test."

Donald shook his head. "I don't believe you. Why would anyone do that?"

Thurman frowned. "Don't be naive, son. This life means nothing to some. You put a switch in front of ten billion people, a switch that kills every one of us the moment you hit it, and you'd have thousands of hands racing to be the one. Tens of thousands. It would only be a matter of time. And that switch *existed*."

"No." Donald flashed back to the first conversation he'd ever had with the senator as a member of Congress, after winning office the first time. It had felt like this, the lies and the truth intermingling and shielding one another. "You'll never convince me," he said. "You'll have to drug me or kill me. You'll never convince me."

Thurman nodded as if he agreed. "Drugging you doesn't work. I've read up on your first shift. There's a small percentage of people with some kind of resistance. I'd love to know why."

Donald laughed. He settled against the wall behind the cot and nestled into the darkness the top bunk provided. "Maybe I've seen too much to forget," he said.

"No, I don't think so." Thurman lowered his head so he could still make eye contact. Donald took a sip of water, both hands wrapped around the glass. "The more you see," Thurman said, "the worse the trauma is, the better it works. Except for some people. Which is why we took a sample."

Donald glanced down at his arm. A small square of gauze had been taped over the spot of blood left by the doctor's needle. He felt a caustic mix of helplessness and fear well up, the mix that moves caged animals to bite at curious hands. "You woke me to take my blood?"

"Not exactly." Thurman hesitated. "Your resistance is something I'm curious about. The reason you're awake is because I was asked to wake you. We're losing silos—"

"I thought that was the plan," Donald spat. "Losing silos. I thought that was what you wanted." He remembered crossing one out with red ink, all those many lives lost. They had accounted for this. Silos were expendable. That's what he'd been told.

Thurman shook his head. "Whatever's happening out there, we need to understand it. And there's someone here who . . . who thinks you may have stumbled onto the answer. A few questions, and then we can put you back under."

Back under. So he wasn't going to be out for long. They woke him to take his blood and to drill into his mind, and then back to sleep. Donald rubbed his arms, which felt thin and atrophied. He was dying in that pod. Only, more slowly than he would like.

"We need to know what you remember about this report." Thurman held it out. Donald waved the thing away.

"I already looked it over," he said. He didn't want to see it again. He could close his eyes and see people spilling out onto the dusty land, a cloud of killing mist, the people that he had ordered dead, more people being trampled inside.

"We have other medications that might ease the—"

"No. No more drugs." Donald crossed his wrists and spread his arms out, slicing the air with both hands. "Look, I don't have a resistance to your drugs." The truth. He was sick of the lies. "There's no mystery. I just stopped taking the pills."

It felt good to admit it. What were they going to do, anyway? Put him back to sleep? That was the answer no matter what. He took another sip of water while he let the confession sink in. He swallowed.

"I kept them in my gums and spat them out later. It's as simple as that. Probably the case with anyone else remembering. Like Hal, or Carlton, or whatever his name was."

Thurman regarded him coolly. He tapped the report against his open palm, seeming to digest this. "We know you stopped taking the pills," he finally said. "And when."

Donald waved his hand. "Mystery solved, then." He finished his water and put the empty glass back on his tray. It felt good to have that out in the open.

"The drugs you have a resistance to are not in the pills, Donny. The reason people stop taking the pills is because they begin to remember, not the other way around."

Donald studied Thurman, disbelieving.

"Your urine changes color when you get off them. You develop sores on your gums. These are the signs we look for."

"What?"

"There are no drugs in the pills, Donny."

"I don't believe you."

"We medicate everyone. There are those of us who are immune. But you shouldn't be."

"Bullshit. I remember. The pills made me woozy. As soon as I stopped taking them, I got better."

Thurman tilted his head to the side. "The reason you stopped taking them was because you were . . . I won't say getting better. It was because the fear had begun leaking through. Donny, the medication is in the water." He waved at the empty glass on the tray. Donald followed the gesture and immediately felt sick, even though he didn't believe him. The suspicion was enough.

"Don't worry," Thurman said. "We'll get to the bottom of it."

"I don't want to help you. I don't want to talk about this report. I don't want to see whoever it is you need me to see."

He wanted Helen. All he wanted was his wife.

"There's a chance that thousands will die if you don't help us. There's a chance that you stumbled onto something with this report of yours, even if I don't believe it."

Donald felt the weight of the soil piled on them both. He glanced at the door to the bathroom, thought about locking himself inside and forcing himself to throw up, to expunge the food and the water.

But it was an insane thought. Maybe Thurman was lying to him. Maybe he was telling the truth. A lie would mean the water was just water. The truth would mean that he did have some sort of resistance. Either way, there was nothing—and everything—to fear.

"I barely remember writing the thing," he admitted. And who would want to see him? He assumed it would be another doctor, maybe a silo head, maybe whoever was running this shift.

He rubbed his temples, could feel the pressure building between them. Maybe he should just do this thing and go back to sleep, back to his skull-filled dreams. Now and then, he had dreamed of Helen. It was the only place left to see her. With this thought, his resistance crumbled like thousand-year-old bones.

"Okay," he said. "I'll go. But I still don't understand what I could possibly know." He rubbed his arm where they'd taken the blood. There was an itch there. An itch so deep it felt like a bruise.

Senator Thurman nodded. "I tend to agree with you. But that's not what she thinks."

Donald stiffened. "She?" He searched Thurman's eyes, wondering if he'd heard correctly. "She who?"

The old man frowned. "The one who had me wake you." He waved his hand at the bunk. "Get some rest. I'll take you to her in the morning."

·8·

He couldn't rest. How could he rest? The hours were cruel, slow, and unknowable. There was no clock to mark their passing, no answer to his frustrated slaps on the door. Donald was left to lie in his bunk and stare at the diamond patterns of interlocking wires holding the mattress above him, to listen to the gurgle of water in hidden pipes as it rushed to another room. He couldn't sleep. He had no idea if it was the middle of the night or the middle of the day. The weight of the silo pressed down. The world was his bunkmate. It lay still as death in the bed above him.

When the boredom grew intolerable, Donald eventually gave in and looked over the report a second time. He studied it more closely. It wasn't the original; the signature was flat, and he remembered using a blue pen. A red marker for the big X on the map and a blue pen for the reports. He was pretty sure.

He skimmed the account of the silo's collapse and his theory that IT heads shadowed too young. His recommendation was to raise the age. He wondered if they had. Maybe so, but the problems were persisting. There was also mention of a young man he had inducted, a young man with a question. His grandmother was one of those who remembered, much like Donald. Like Hal or Carter or whatever his name had been. Donald had suggested in the report that entertaining one question from inductees might be a good idea. They were given the Legacy, after all. Their cruel test was a severe application of the truth. Why not show them, in that final stage of indoctrination, that there were more truths to be had?

It had seemed like a good idea at the time, but Donald remembered being a mess when he wrote the report. Maybe it had been his own questions, his own need for answers, that had driven him to suggest this.

The tiny clicks of a key entering a lock. Thurman opened the door as Donald folded the report away.

"How're you feeling?" Thurman asked.

Donald didn't say.

"Can you walk?"

He nodded. A walk. When what he really wanted was to run screaming down the hallway, to kick things over and punch holes in walls. But a walk would do. A walk before his next long nap.

• • • •

They rode the elevator in silence. Donald noticed Thurman had scanned his badge before pressing one of the shiny buttons, level fifty-four. Its number stood bright and new while so many others had been worn away. There was nothing but supplies on that level if Donald remembered correctly, supplies they weren't supposed to ever need. The lift slowed as it approached a level it normally skipped. The doors opened on a cavernous expanse of shelves stocked with instruments of death.

Thurman led him down the middle of it all. There were wooden crates with "AMMO" stenciled on the side, longer crates beside them with military designations like "M22" and "M19" that Donald recognized as being guns. Not that he knew what those guns looked like or how to operate them, but he had been to movies, and like any other young boy he had known what to call his stick while he fired imaginary bullets at his friends.

More shelves with armor and helmets, with supplies, some boxes unlabeled. And beyond the shelves, tarps that covered bulbous and winged forms that he knew to be drones. UAVs. His sister had flown them in a war that now seemed pointless and distant, part of ancient history. But here these relics stood, oiled and covered, waiting, both proud and paranoid, confident and reeking of grease and fear.

Beyond the drones, Thurman led the way through a murky dimness that made the wide storehouse seem to go on forever. Donald padded quietly behind, fearful of waking these demon sentinels, this aviary that promised hell-rain from the skies.

At the far end of the wide room, a hallway leaked a glow of light. An arrangement of offices, a wall lined with filing cabinets spotted with dots of rust, not greased like the other things. And in one wide room, the sounds of paper stirring, a chair squeaking as someone turned. Thurman rapped his knuckles on the doorframe. Donald rounded the corner and saw, inexplicably, *her* sitting there.

"Anna?"

He remained frozen in the doorway. Anna sat behind a huge conference table ringed with identical chairs. She looked up from a wide spread of paperwork and a computer monitor. There was no shock on her part, just a smile of acknowledgment and a weariness that the smile could not conceal.

Her father crossed the room while Donald gaped. Thurman squeezed her arm and kissed her on the cheek, but Anna's eyes did not leave Donald's. The old man whispered something to his daughter, then announced that he had work of his own to see to. Donald did not budge until the Senator had left the room, the armory swallowing an old soldier's footsteps.

"Anna—"

She was already around the massive table, wrapping her arms around him. Donald sagged into her embrace, suddenly exhausted. She was whispering things, the sing-song tunes of placating mothers, the there-theres and shushes. It took this to inform Donald that he was shaking. He felt her hand come down the back of his head and rest on his neck, his own arms crossing her back like a spring-loaded habit. Here was why women didn't pull shifts. Here was a truth the shrinks knew. Donald could feel himself grow both weak and bold. He had dangerous thoughts of giving in and more dangerous thoughts of lashing out. Here was the love and violence in the hearts of men, all for their women.

"What're you doing here?" he whispered. Did she not know the danger? The disruptive power of her gender? And what weakness was this of a father to wake a child in the middle of a storm?

"I'm here for the same reason you are." She pulled back from the embrace. "I'm looking for answers." She stepped away and surveyed the mess on the table. "To different questions, perhaps."

Donald finally saw what the table was, what the *room* was. A familiar schematic—a grid of silos—covered the table. Each silo was like a small plate, all of them trapped under the glass. A dozen chairs were gathered around. It was a war room, where generals stood and pushed plastic models and grumbled over lives lost by the thousands. He glanced up at the maps and schematics plastered on the walls. There was an adjoining bathroom, a towel hanging from a hook on the door. A cot had been set up in the far corner and was neatly made. There was a lamp beside it sitting on one of the wooden crates from the storeroom. Extension cords snaked here and there, signs of a room long converted into an apartment of sorts.

Donald wanted desperately to fall into the cot. He looked to Anna, made sure she was still there, and in a disturbed corner of his mind he thought this meant Helen must also be somewhere that he could wake her. Life, death, sleeping, rising, the passage of time, the workings of his own mind—all of it was soft and without meaning.

He turned to the nearest wall and flipped through some of the drawings. They were three layers deep in places and covered in notes. It didn't look like a war was being planned. It looked like a scene from the crime shows that used to lull him to sleep in a former life.

"You've been up longer than me," he said.

Anna stood beside him. Her hand lighted on his shoulder like a bird, and Donald felt himself startle to be touched at all.

"Almost a year, now." Her hand slid down his back before falling away. "Can I get you a drink? Water? I also have a stash of scotch down here. Dad doesn't know half the stuff they hid away in these crates."

Donald shook his head. He turned and watched as she disappeared into the bathroom and ran the sink. She emerged, sipping from a glass.

"What's going on here?" he asked. "Why am I up?"

She swallowed and waved her glass at the walls. "It's—" She laughed and shook her head. "I was about to say it's nothing, but this is the hell that keeps me out of one box and in another. It doesn't concern you, most of this."

Donald studied the room again. He could feel the dark halls of shelves and crates stretching back toward the elevator. A year, living like this. He turned his attention to Anna, the way her hair was balled up in a bun, a pen sticking out of it. Her skin was pale except for the dark rings beneath her eyes. He wondered how she was able to do this, live like this.

There was a printout on the far wall that matched the table, a grid of circles, the layout of the facilities. A familiar red X had been drawn across what he knew to be Silo 12 in the upper left corner. There was another X nearby, a new one. More lives lost while he slept. Thousands screaming while in his nightmares he could make no sound. And in the lower right-hand corner of the grid, a mess that made no sense. The room seemed to wobble a bit as he took a step closer.

"Donny?"

"What happened here?" he asked, his voice a whisper. Anna turned to see what he was looking at. She glanced at the table, and he realized that her paperwork was scattered around the same corner of the facility. The glass surface crawled with notes written in red and blue wax.

"Donny—" She stepped closer. "Things aren't well."

He turned and studied the scrawl of red marks on the wall schematic. There were Xs and question marks. There were notes in red ink with lines and arrows. Ten or a dozen of the silos were marked up to hell.

"How many?" he asked, trying to count, to multiply the thousands. "Are they gone?"

She took a deep breath. "We don't know." She finished her water, walked down the long line of chairs pushed up against the table, and reached down into the seat of one. She procured a bottle and poured a few fingers into her plastic cup. *Better than a blue pill,* Donald thought.

"It started with Silo 40," she said. "It went dark about a year ago—"

"Went dark?"

Anna took a sip of the scotch and nodded. She licked her lips. "The camera feeds went out first. Not at once, but eventually they got them all. We lost contact with the heads over there. Couldn't raise anyone. Erskine was running the shift at the time. He followed the Order and gave the okay to shut the silo down—"

"You mean kill everyone."

Anna shot him a look. "You know what had to be done."

Donald remembered Silo 12. He remembered making that same decision. As if there had been a decision to make. The system was automatic, wasn't it? Wasn't he just doing what came next, following a set of procedures written down by someone else? He remembered a debate from a history class in college, a group of students arguing that the first president to drop a bomb hadn't had any other choice. All that time and money invested, the military saying this was the only way. What was heroic or brave about carrying out the inevitable? What kind of man would it have taken to have bucked the expected? What if he hadn't aborted Silo 12? What if those people had scurried over the hills and had realized they weren't alone? Who would be the hero then? Who the villain?

He studied the poster with the red marks. "And the rest of them? The other silos?"

Anna finished the drink with one long pull and gasped for air afterward. Donald caught her eyeing the bottle. "They woke up Dad when 42 went. Two more silos had gone dark by the time he came for me—"

Two more silos. "Why you?" he asked.

She tucked a strand of loose hair behind her ear. "Because there was no one else. Because everyone who had a hand in designing this place was either gone or at their wits' end. Because Dad was desperate."

"He wanted to see you."

She laughed. "It wasn't that. Trust me." She waved her empty cup at the arrangement of circles on the table and the spread of papers. "They were using the radios at high frequencies. We think it started with 40, that maybe their IT Head went rogue. They hijacked their antenna and began communicating with the other silos around them, and we couldn't cut them off. They had taken care of that as well. As soon as Dad suspected this, he argued with the others that wireless networks were my specialty. They eventually relented."

"The others? Who all knows you're here?" Donald couldn't help but think how dangerous this could get, but maybe that was his own weakness screaming at him.

"My dad, Erskine, Dr. Henson, his assistants who brought me out. But those assistants won't work another shift—"

"Deep freeze?"

Anna frowned and splashed her cup, and it occurred to Donald how much could take place while a man slept. Entire shifts had gone by. Another silo had been lost, another red X drawn on the map. An entire corner of silos had run into some kind of trouble. Thurman, meanwhile, had been awake for a year, dealing with it. His daughter as well. So much had happened while Donald had dreamt of snarling dogs with bat-like wings and piles of bones. He waved his arm at the room. "You've been stuck in here for a year. Working on this."

She jerked her head at the door and laughed. "I've been cooped up in worse for a lot longer. But yeah, it sucks. I'm sick of this place." She took another sip, her cup hiding her expression, and Donald wondered if perhaps he was awake because of her weakness just as she might be awake because of her father's. What was next? Him searching the deep freeze for his sister Charlotte? How would it end?

"We've lost contact with eleven silos so far." Anna peered into her cup. "I think I've got it contained, but we're still trying to figure out how it happened or if anyone's still alive over there. I don't think so, but Dad wants to send scouts. Others say that's a bigger risk. And now it looks like 18 is going to burn itself to the ground."

"And I'm supposed to help? What does your dad think I know?" He stepped around the planning table and waved for the bottle. Anna splashed her cup and handed the drink to him; she reached for another cup by her monitor while Donald collapsed onto her cot. It was a lot to take in.

"It's not Dad who thinks you know anything. He didn't want you up at all. No one's supposed to come out of deep freeze." She screwed the cap back on the bottle. "It was his boss."

Donald nearly choked on his first sip of the scotch. He sputtered and wiped his chin with his sleeve while Anna looked on with concern.

"His *boss?*" he asked, gasping for air.

She narrowed her eyes. "Dad told you why you're here, right?"

He fumbled in his pocket for the report. "Something I wrote during my last . . . during my shift. Thurman has a boss? I thought he was in charge."

Anna laughed, but there was no humor there. "Nobody's in charge," she told him. "The system's in charge. It just runs. We built it to just *go*." She got up from her desk and studied something on the wall for a moment, then walked over and joined him on the cot, the springs squeaking in complaint. Donald slid over to give her more room.

"Dad was in charge of digging the holes, that was his job. There were three of them who planned most of this. The other two had ideas for how to hide this place. Dad convinced them they should just build it in plain sight. The nuclear containment facility was his idea, and he was in a position to make it happen."

A flood of memories washed over Donald. He remembered being convinced to run for office. Was it Mick who had goaded him into it? Or was it Thurman?

"You said three. Who were the others?"

"Victor and Erskine." Anna adjusted a pillow and leaned back against the wall. "Not their real names, of course. But what does it matter? A name is a name. You can be anyone down here. Erskine was the one who discovered the original threat, who told Victor and Dad about the nanos. You'll meet him. He's been on a double shift with me, working on the loss of these silos, but it's out of his area of expertise. Do you need more?" She nodded at his cup.

"No. I'm already feeling dizzy." He didn't add that it wasn't from the alcohol. "I remember a Victor from my shift. He worked across the hall from me."

"The same." She looked away for a moment. "Dad refers to him as the boss, but I've been working with Victor for a while, and he never thought of himself that way. He thought of himself as a steward, joked once about feeling like Noah. He wanted to wake you months ago because of this Silo 18, but Dad vetoed the idea. I think Victor was fond of you. He talked about you a lot."

"Victor talked about *me?*" Donald remembered the man across the hall from him, the shrink. Anna reached up and wiped at the bottom of her eyes.

"Yes. He was a brilliant man, could tell what you were thinking, what anyone was thinking. He planned most of this. Wrote the Order, the original Pact. It was all his design."

"What do you mean *was?*"

Her lip trembled. She tipped her cup, but there was little solace left in it.

"Victor's dead," she said. "He shot himself at his desk two days ago."

· 9 ·

"Victor? Shot himself?" Donald tried to imagine the composed man who had worked across the hall from him doing such a thing. "Why?"

Anna sniffed and slid closer to Donald. She twisted the empty cup in her hands. "We don't know. He was obsessed with that first silo we lost. Obsessed. It broke my heart to see how he blamed himself. He used to say that he could see certain things coming, that there were . . . probabilistic certainties." She said these two words in a mimic of his voice, which brought the old man's face even more vividly to Donald's mind.

"But it killed him not to know the precise when and where." She dabbed her eyes. "He would've been better off if it'd happened on someone else's shift. Not his. Not where he'd feel guilty."

"He blamed me," Donald said, staring at the floor. "It was on my shift. I was such a mess. I couldn't think straight."

"What? No. Donny, no." She rested a hand on his knee. "There's no one to blame."

"But my report—" He still had it in his hand, folded up and dotted here and there with pale blue.

Anna's eyes fell to the piece of paper. "Is that a copy?" She sniffed and reached for it, brushed the loose strands of hair off her face. "Dad had the courage to tell you about this but not about what Vic did." She shook her head. "Victor was strong in some ways, so weak in others." She turned to Donald. "He was found at his desk, surrounded by notes, everything he had on this silo, and your report was on top."

She unfolded the page and studied the words. "Just a copy," she whispered.

"Maybe it was—" Donald began.

"He wrote notes all over his copy." She slid her finger across the page. "Right about here, he wrote '*This is why.*'"

"This is why? As in why he did it?" Donald waved his hand at the room. "Shouldn't *this* be why? Maybe he realized he'd made a mistake." He held Anna's arm. "Think about what we've done. What if we followed a crazy man down here? Maybe Victor had a sudden bout of *sanity*. What if he woke up for a second and saw what we'd done?"

"No." Anna shook her head. "We had to do this."

He slapped the wall behind the cot. "That's what everyone keeps saying."

"Listen to me." She placed a hand on his knee, tried to soothe him. "You need to keep it together, okay?" She glanced toward the door, a fearful look in her eyes. "I asked him to wake you because I need your help. I can't do all of this alone. Vic was working on Silo 18. If it's up to Dad, he'll just terminate the place not to have to deal with it. Victor didn't want that. *I* don't want that."

Donald thought of Silo 12, which he'd terminated. But it was already falling, wasn't it? It was already too late. They had opened the airlock. He looked toward the schematic on the wall and wondered if it was too late for this silo as well. Maybe when they put him down again, maybe he would dream better dreams if this place could be saved. Maybe the pile of bones would have a summit this time.

"What did he see in my report?" he asked.

"I don't know. But he wanted to see you weeks ago. He thought you touched on something."

"Or maybe it was just because I was around at the time."

Donald looked at the room of clues. Anna had been digging, tearing into a different problem. So many questions and answers. His mind was clear, not like last time. He had questions of his own. He wanted to find his sister, find out what happened to Helen, dispel this crazy thought that she was still out there somewhere. He wanted to know more about this damnable place he'd helped build.

"You'll help us?" Anna asked. She rested her hand on his back. Her touch was comforting for a moment, and then he thought of Helen. He startled as if bit, some wild part of him thinking for a moment that he was still married, that she was alive out there, maybe frozen and waiting for him to wake her.

"I need—" He stood and glanced around the room. His eyes fell to the computer on the desk. "I need to look some things up."

Anna rose beside him. She fumbled for his hand. "Of course. I can fill you in with what we know so far. Victor left a series of notes. He wrote all over your report. I can show you. And maybe you can convince Dad that he was onto something, that this silo is worth saving—"

"Yes," Donald said. He would do it. But only so he could stay awake. That was his motivation. And he wondered for a moment if it was Anna's as well. To keep him around.

An hour ago, all he had wanted was to go back to sleep, to escape the world he had helped create. But now he wanted answers. He would look into this silo with its problems, but he would find Helen as well. Find out what'd happened to her, where she was. He thought of Mick, and Tennessee flashed in his mind. He turned toward the wall schematic with all the silos, tried to remember which state went with which number.

"What can we access from here?" he asked. His skin flushed with heat as he thought of the answers at his disposal. Maybe this computer wouldn't be locked down like his last one. No games of solitaire to subdue curious minds.

Anna turned toward the door. There were footsteps out there in the darkness.

"Dad. He's the only one with access to this level anymore."

"Anymore?" He turned back to Anna.

"Yeah. Where do you think Victor got the gun?" She lowered her voice. "I was in here when he came down and cracked open one of the crates. I never heard him. Look, my father blames himself for what happened, and he still doesn't believe this has anything to do with you or your report. But I know Vic. He wasn't crazy. If there's anything you can do, please. For me."

She squeezed his hand. Donald looked down, didn't realize she'd been holding it. The folded report was in her other hand. The footsteps approached. Donald nodded his assent.

"Thank you," she said. She dropped his hand, grabbed his empty cup from the cot, and nested hers with it. The cups and the bottle were tucked into one of the chairs, which slid against the table as Thurman arrived at the door and rapped the jamb with his knuckles.

"Come in," Anna said, brushing loose hair off her face.

Thurman studied the two of them a moment. "Erskine is planning a small ceremony," he said. "Just us. Those of us who know."

Anna nodded. "Of course."

Thurman narrowed his eyes and glanced from his daughter to Donald. Anna seemed to take it as a question.

"He thinks he can help," she said. "We both think it's best for him to work down here with me. At least until we make some progress."

Donald turned to her in shock. Thurman said nothing.

"We'll need another computer," she added. "If you bring one down, I can set it up."

That, Donald liked the sound of.

"And another cot, of course," Anna added with a smile.

• Silo 18 •

Hush-a-bye baby
in the Up Top
When the wind blows,
the cradle will rock.
When the dust comes,
the cradle will fall.
And down will come baby,
Silo and All.

-Jennifer Plume, age 17

·10·

Mission slunk away after the fight with the farmers as the rest of the porters scattered. He stole a few hours of sleep at the upper waystation, his nose numb and lips throbbing from a blow he'd suffered. Tossing and turning, too restless to stay put, he rose in the dim-time and realized it was early yet to go to the Nest. The Crow would still be asleep. And so he headed to the cafeteria for a sunrise and a decent breakfast, the coroner's bonus burning in his pockets the way his knuckles burned from their scrapes.

He nursed his aches with a welcomed hot meal, eating with those coming off a midnight shift, and watched the clouds boil and come to life across the hills. The towering husks in the distance—the Crow called them buildings—were the first to catch the rising sun. It was a sign that the world would wake one more day. His birthday, Mission realized. And he regretted coming up there. He left his dishes on the table, a chit for whoever cleaned after him, and tried not to think of cleaning at all. Instead, he rushed down the eight flights of stairs before the silo fully woke. He headed toward the Nest, feeling not a day older at all.

Familiar words greeted him at the landing of the eighth. There, above the door, rather than a level number it read:

The Crow's Nest

The words were painted in bright and blocky letters. They followed the outlines from years and generations prior, color piled on color, letters crooked and bent from more than one young hand's involvement. Where the paint had gone outside the lines, silo gray had been slapped on top to try and cover it up.

Mission remembered helping with the latest coat. Another would be needed soon. Already, a prior color from another age could be seen through the blues and purples that he and his friends had chosen. And where the blue paint was thin and the color beneath had chipped away, a third layer could be seen beyond. It was like peering into the past. For all he knew, there could be five or six layers hidden beneath. The children of the silo came and went and left their marks with bristles, but the Old Crow remained.

Her nest comprised the nursery, day school, and classrooms that served the Up Top. She had been perched there for longer than any alive could remember. Some said she was as old as the silo itself, but Mission knew that was just a legend. He'd heard it said that the limits to the silo were the limits to life, that no one could ever reach a hundred and fifty in age. This, he believed. His uncle had been one third that when he died. Most people never reached half the levels in age. But the Crow wasn't most people.

He passed beneath the door and reached up to slap the paint as he went. A small hop where terrible leaps were once needed. He remembered employing a ladder before that, spilling a bucket of blue paint, hearing the complaints from Fourteen as it dribbled down. Maybe that's where the idea for the plasticwrap paintbombs had come from. It must've been. Kids playing at the wars their fathers had fought. Screams fading to laughter over time—warlike grunts into giggles—chasing each other with imaginary weapons and kitchen utensils, fighting over who got to be Security and who had to play the bad guys.

Mission remembered how exciting those adventures had felt. Such joyous times now seemed sad as they became truer and truer.

He entered the Nest to find the hallways empty and quiet, the hour early still. There was a soft screech from one classroom as desks were put back into order. Mission caught a glimpse of two teachers conferring in another classroom, their faces scrunched up with worry, probably wondering what to do with a younger version of himself. The scent of strong tea mixed with the odor of paste and chalk. There were rows of metal lockers in dire need of paint and stippled with dents from tiny fists; they transported Mission back to another age. Just yesterday, he was terrorizing that hall. He and all his friends whom he didn't see anymore—not as often as he'd like.

The Crow's room was at the far end adjoining the only apartment on the entire level. The apartment had been built especially for her, converted from a classroom, or so they said. And while she only taught the youngest children anymore, the entire school was hers. This was her nest, her aerie.

Mission remembered coming to her at various stages of his life. Early on, for comfort, feeling so very far from the farms. Later, for wisdom, when he was finally old enough to admit he had none. And more than once he had come for both, like the day he had learned the truth of his birth and his mother's death—that she had been sent to clean because of him. Mission remembered that day well. It was the only time he'd seen the Old Crow cry.

He knocked on her classroom door before entering and found her at the blackboard that'd been lowered so she could write on it from her chair. Mrs. Crowe stopped erasing yesterday's lessons, turned, and beamed at him.

"My boy," she croaked. She smiled and waved with the eraser to beckon him closer, a chalky haze filling the air. "My boy, my boy."

"Hello, Mrs. Crowe." Mission passed through the handful of desks to get to her. The power line for her electric chair drooped from the center of the ceiling to the pole that rose up from the chair's back. Mission ducked beneath it as he got closer and bent to give the Crow a hug. His hands wrapped around her and the chair both, and her smell was one of childhood and innocence. The yellow gown she wore, spotted with flowers, was her Wednesday fare, as good as any calendar. It had faded since Mission's time, as all things had.

"I do believe you've grown," she said, smiling up at him. Her voice was a bare whisper, and he recalled how it kept even the young ones quiet as death so they could hear what was being said. She brought her hand up and touched her own cheek. "What happened to your face?"

Mission laughed and shrugged off his porter's pack. "Just an accident," he said, lying to her like old times. He placed his pack at the foot of one of the tiny desks, could imagine squeezing into the thing and staying for the day's lesson. He noticed only a handful of the chairs were arranged for use. The rest were shoved against the back wall, waiting for the next boom, the next surge in population.

"How've you been?" he asked. He studied her face, the deep wrinkles and dark skin like a farmer's but from age rather than grow lights. Her eyes were rheumy, but there was a life behind them.

They reminded Mission of the wallscreens on a bright day but in dire need of a cleaning.

"Not so good," Mrs. Crowe said. She twisted the lever on her armrest, and the chair built for her decades ago by some long-gone former student whirred around to better face him. Pulling back her sleeve, she showed Mission a gauze bandage taped to her thin and splotchy arm. "Those doctors came and took my blood away!" Her hand shook as she indicated the evidence. "Took half of it, by my reckoning."

Mission laughed. "I'm pretty sure they didn't take half your blood, Mrs. Crowe. The doctors are just looking out for you."

She twisted up her face, an explosion of wrinkles like a palm as it closed into a fist. She didn't seem so sure. "I don't trust them," she said.

Mission smiled. "You don't trust anyone. And hey, maybe they're just trying to figure out why you can't die like everyone else does. Maybe they'll come up with a way for everyone to live as long as you some day."

Mrs. Crowe rubbed the bandage on her withering arm. "Or they're sorting out how to *kill* me," she said.

"Oh, don't be so sinister." Mission reached forward and pulled her sleeve down to keep her from messing with the bandage. "Why would you think such a thing?"

She frowned and declined to answer. Her eyes fell to his sagging and mostly empty pack. "Day off?" she asked.

Mission turned and followed her gaze. "Hmm? Oh, no. I dropped off last night. I'll pick up another delivery in a little bit, take it wherever they tell me to."

"Oh, to be so young and free again." Mrs. Crowe spun her chair around and steered it behind her desk. Mission ducked beneath the pivoting wire out of habit; the pole at the back of the chair was made with younger heads in mind. She picked up a container of the vile vegetable pulp she preferred over water and took a sip. "Allie stopped by last week." She set the greenish-black fluid down. "She was asking about you. Wanted to know if you were still single."

"Oh?" Mission could feel his temperature shoot up. Mrs. Crowe had caught them kissing once, back before he knew what kissing was for. She had left them with a warning and a knowing smile. "I saw Jenine yesterday," Mission said, changing the subject, hoping she might take the hint. "Everyone's so spread out."

"As it should be." The Crow opened a drawer on her desk and rummaged around, came out with an envelope. Mission could see a half-dozen names scratched out across the thing. It'd been used a handful of times. "You're heading down from here? Maybe you could drop off something for Rodny?"

She held out the letter. Mission took it, saw his best friend's name written on the outside, all the other names crossed out.

"I can leave it for him, sure. The last two times I stopped by there, they said he was unavailable."

Mrs. Crowe nodded as if this was to be expected. "Ask for Jeffery, he's the head of security down there, one of my boys. You tell him that this is from me and that I said you should hand it to Rodny yourself. In person." She waved her hands in the air, little trembling blurs. "I'll write Jeffery a note."

Mission glanced up at the clock on the wall while she dug into her desk for a pen and ink. Soon, the hallways would begin filling with youthful chatter and the opening and slamming of lockers. He waited patiently while she scratched her note. In the while, he scanned the walls at the old motivators, as Mrs. Crowe like to call the posters and banners she made.

You can be anything, one of them said. It featured a crude drawing of a boy and a girl standing on a huge mound. The mound was green and the sky blue, just like in the picture books. Another one said: *Dream to your heart's delight.* It had bands of color in a graceful sweep. The Crow had a name for the shape, but he'd forgotten what it was called. Another familiar one: *Go new places.* It featured a drawing of a crow perched in an impossibly large tree, it's wings spread as if it were about to take flight.

"Jeffery is the bald one," Mrs. Crowe said. She waved a hand over her own white and thinning hair to demonstrate.

"I know the one," Mission said. It was a strange reminder that so many of the adults and elders throughout the silo had been her students as well. A locker was slammed in the hallway. Mission remembered when he was a kid how the rows and rows of tiny desks had filled the room. There were cubbies full of rolled mats for nap time, reminding him of the daily routine of clearing a space in the middle of the floor, finding his mat, and drifting off to sleep while the Crow sang to them. He missed those days. He missed the Old Time stories about a world full of impossible things. Leaning against that little desk, Mission suddenly felt as ancient as the Crow, just as impossibly distant from his youth.

"Give Jeffery this, and then see that Rodny gets my note. From you personally, okay?"

He grabbed his pack and slid both pieces of correspondence into his courier pouch. There was no mention of payment, just the twinge of guilt Mission felt for even thinking it. Digging into the pack reminded him of the items he had brought her, forgotten due to the previous night's brawl.

"Oh, I brought you these from the farm." He pulled out a few small cucumbers, two peppers, and a large tomato. He placed them on her desk. "For your veggie drinks," he said.

Mrs. Crowe clasped her hands together and smiled with delight.

"Is there anything else you need next time I'm passing by?"

"These visits," she said, her face a wrinkle of smiles. "All I care about are my little ones. Stop by whenever you can, okay?"

Mission squeezed her arm, which felt like a broomstick tucked into a sleeve. "I will," he said. "And that reminds me: Jenine, Frankie, and Steven all told me to tell you hello. And I'm probably forgetting someone."

"Those boys should come more often," she told him, her voice a quiver.

"Not everyone gets around like I do," he said. "I'm sure they'd like to see you more often as well."

"You tell them," she said. "Tell them I don't have much time left—"

Mission laughed and waved off the morbid thought. "You probably told my grandfather the same thing when he was young, and his father before him."

The Crow smiled as if this were true. "Predict the inevitable," she said, "and you're bound to be right one day."

Mission smiled. He liked that. "Still, I wish you wouldn't talk about dying. Nobody likes to hear it."

"They may not like it, but a reminder is good." She held out her arms, the sleeves of her flowered dress falling away and revealing the bandage once more. "Tell me, what do you see when you look at these hands?" She turned them over, back and forth. She studied them as if they belonged to another.

"I see time," Mission blurted out, not sure where the thought came from. He tore his eyes away, suddenly finding her skin to be grotesque. Like shriveled potatoes found deep in the soil long after harvest time. He hated himself for feeling it.

"Time, sure," Mrs. Crowe said. "There's time here aplenty. But there's *remnants*, too. I remember things being better, once. You think on the bad to remind yourself of the good."

She studied her hands a moment longer as if looking for something else. When she lifted her gaze and peered at Mission, her eyes were shining with sadness. Mission could feel his own eyes watering, partly from discomfort, partly due to the somber pall that had been cast like a cold and wet blanket over the conversation. It reminded him that today was his birthday, a thought that tightened his neck and emptied his chest. He was sure the Crow knew what day it was. She just loved him enough not to say.

"I was beautiful, once, you know." Mrs. Crowe withdrew her hands and folded them in her lap. "Once that's gone, once it leaves us for good, no one will ever see it again."

Mission felt a powerful urge to soothe her, to tell Mrs. Crowe that she was still beautiful in plenty of ways. She could still make music. Could paint. Few others remembered how. She could make children feel loved and safe, another bit of magic long forgotten.

"When I was your age," the Crow said, smiling, "I could have any boy I wanted."

She laughed, dispelling the tension and casting away the shadows that had fallen over their talk, but Mission believed her. He believed her even though he couldn't picture it, couldn't imagine away the wrinkles and the spots and the long strands of hair on her knuckles. Still, he believed her. He always did.

"The world is a lot like me, you know." She lifted her gaze toward the ceiling and perhaps beyond. "The world was beautiful once, too."

Mission sensed an Old Time story brewing like a storm of clouds. More lockers were slammed in the hallway, little voices gathering.

"Tell me," Mission said, remembering the hours that had passed like eyeblinks at her feet, the songs she sang while children slept. "Tell me about the old world."

The Old Crow's eyes narrowed and settled on a dark corner of the room. A deep breath rattled in her once-proud chest. Her lips, furrowed with the wrinkles of time, parted, and a story began, a story Mission had heard a thousand times before. But it never got old, visiting this land of the Crow's imagination. And as the little ones skipped into the room, they too fell silent and gathered around. They slipped into their tiny desks and followed along with the widest of eyes and the most open of unknowing minds these tales of a world, once beautiful, and now fairly forgotten.

·11·

The stories Mrs. Crowe made up were straight from the children's books. There were blue skies and lands of green, white clouds and rainbows, animals like dogs and cats but bigger than people. Juvenile stuff. And yet, these fantastic tales of a better place somewhere impossibly distant left Mission feeling angry at the world he was stuck with. He thought this as he left the Up Top behind and wound his way past the farms and the levels of his youth. The promise of an *elsewhere* highlighted the flaws of the familiar. He had gone off to be a porter, to fly away and be all that he wished, and what he wished was to be further away than this world would allow.

These were dangerous thoughts. They reminded him of his mother and where she had been sent seventeen years ago to the day.

Past the farms, Mission noted something burning further down the silo. The air was hazy, and there was the bitter tinge of smoke on the back of his tongue. A trash pile, maybe. Someone who didn't want to pay the fee to have it ported to recycling. Or someone who didn't think the silo would be around long enough to *need* to recycle.

It could be an accident, of course. It could be a legitimate danger. But that's not where Mission's mind went. Nobody thought that way anymore. He could see it on the faces of those on the stairwell. He could see by the way belongings were clutched, children sheltered, that the future of everything was in doubt. There hadn't been nearly as much new graffiti lately. Even the delinquents had begun to wonder: *What's the point?*

Mission adjusted his light pack and hurried down to the IT levels. He remembered his father's talk of restoring the silo after the last outbreak of violence. There were physical things to patch, like the stairwell, but the population, too. Physical explosions led to population explosions. Record numbers of lottery winners followed the fighting. His father spoke of so many bodies to dispose of that the airlock had been employed, the great flames cremating the dead by the score, their ashes set loose to blur the view. It made clear the link between life and death, that each birth was owed to another's passing. The difference with Mission was that he *knew* who that other person was.

He reached IT and pushed his way through a crowd on landing thirty-four. It was mostly boys his age or a little older, many that he recognized, a lot from the mids. Several who didn't match this profile stood with computers tucked under their arms, wires dangling, jostling with the rest. Mission picked his way through the throng. A computer was dropped, which led to shouting and shoving. Inside, he found a barrier had been set up just beyond the door. Two men from Security manned the temporary gate and allowed only crumpled IT workers through.

"Delivery," Mission shouted. He worked his way to the front, carefully extracting the note Mrs. Crowe had written. "Delivery for Officer Jeffery."

One of the security men took the note. Mission was pressed against the barrier by those behind. A woman who belonged was waved through. She hurried toward the proper security gate leading into the main hall, smoothing her coveralls with obvious relief. There were crowds of young men being given instructions in one corner of the wide hall. They stood at attention in neat rank and file, but their eyes were wide as the stairwell.

"What the hell is going on?" Mission asked, as the barrier was parted for him.

"What the hell isn't?" one of the security guards rejoined. "Power spike last night took out a load of computers. Every one of our techs is pulling a double. There's a fire down in Mechanical or something, and some kinda violence up in the farms. Did you get the wire?"

Mechanical. That was a long way away to nose a fire. And word was out about last night's raid, making him self-conscious of the cut on his nose. "What wire?" he asked.

The security guard pointed to the groups of boys. "We're hiring. New techs."

All Mission saw were young men, and the guy talking to them was with Security, not IT. The security guard handed back the note to Mission and pointed toward the main security gate. The woman from earlier was already beeping her way through, a large and familiar bald head swiveling to watch her ass as she headed down the hall.

"Thanks," Mission said to the guard, hurrying away from the crush of people. "Sir?" he called out as he approached the gate.

Jeffery turned his head, the deep wrinkles and folds of flesh disappearing from his neck.

"Hmm? Oh—" he snapped his fingers, trying to place the name. "Mission."

He wagged his finger. "That's right. You need to leave something with me, porter?" He held out a palm but seemed disinterested.

Mission handed him the note. "Actually, I have orders from Mrs. Crowe to deliver it in person." He pulled the sealed envelope with the crossed-out names from his courier pouch. "Just a letter, sir."

The old guard glanced at the envelope, then continued reading the note addressed to him. "Rodny isn't available." He shook his head. "I can't give you a timeframe, either. Could be weeks. You wanna leave it with me?"

Again, an outstretched palm; this time with more interest. Mission pulled the envelope back warily. "I can't. There's no way I can just hand it to him? This is the Crow, man. If it were the Mayor asking me, I'd say no problem."

Jeffery smiled. "You were one of her boys, too?"

Mission nodded. The head of Security looked past him at a man approaching the gate with his ID out. Mission stepped aside as the gentleman scanned his way through, nodding good morning to Jeffery.

"Tell you what. I'm taking Rodny his lunch in a little bit. When I do, you can come with me, hand him the letter with me standing there, and I won't have to worry about the Crow nipping my hide later. How's that sound?"

Mission smiled. "Sounds good, man. I appreciate it."

The officer pointed across the noisy entrance hall. "Why don't you go grab yourself some water and hang in the conference room.

There's some boys in there filling out paperwork." Jeffery looked Mission up and down. "In fact, why don't you fill out an application? We could use you."

"I . . . uh, don't know much about computers," Mission said.

Jeffery shrugged as if that were irrelevant. "Suit yourself. One of the boys will be relieving me in a little bit. I'll come get you."

Mission thanked him again. He crossed the large entrance hall where neat columns and rows of young men listened to barked instructions. Another guard waved him inside the conference room while holding out a sheet of paper and a shard of charcoal. Mission saw that the back of the paper was blank and took it with no plan for filling it out. Half a chit right there in usable paper.

There were a few empty chairs around the wide table. He chose one. A number of boys scribbled with their charcoals on the pages, faces scrunched up in concentration. Mission sat with his back to the only window and placed his sack on the wide table, kept the letter in his hands. The application he slid inside his pack for future use. He studied for the first time the Crow's letter.

The envelope was old but addressed only a handful of times. One edge was worn tissue thin, a small tear revealing a folded piece of paper inside. Peering closer, Mission saw that it was pulp paper, probably made in the Crow's Nest by one of her kids, water and handfuls of torn paper blended up and pressed down on screens and left overnight to dry. Bits of thread and various colors could be seen in there, and just the hint of writing.

"Mission," someone at the table hissed.

He looked up to see Bradley sitting across from him. The fellow porter had his blue 'chief tied around his bicep. Mission had thought he was running a regular route in the Down Deep.

"You applying?" Bradley hissed.

One of the other boys coughed into his fist like he was asking for quiet. It looked like Bradley was already done with his application.

Mission shook his head. There was a knock on the window behind him, and he nearly dropped the letter as he whirled around. Jeffery stuck his head in the door. "Two minutes," he said to Mission, ignoring the other lads. He jabbed his thumb over his shoulder. "I'm just waiting on his tray."

Mission bobbed his head as the door was pulled shut. The other boys looked at him curiously.

"Delivery," Mission explained to Bradley loud enough for the others to hear. He pulled his pack closer and hid the envelope behind it. The boys went back to their scribbling. Bradley frowned and watched the others.

Mission studied the envelope again. Two minutes. How long would he have with Rodny? He tickled the corner of the sealed flap. The milk paste the Crow had used didn't stick very well to the months-old—maybe years-old—dried glue from before. He worked one corner loose without glancing down at the envelope. Instead, he watched Bradley as he disobeyed the third cardinal rule of porting, telling himself this was different, that this was two old friends talking and he was just in the room with them. Just friends talking as he peeled the flap away.

Even so, his hands trembled as he pulled the letter out. He glanced down, keeping the note hidden. Purple and red string lay strewn in with the dark gray of cheap paper. Kid paper. The writing was in chalk. It meant the words had to be big. White powder gathered in the folds as it shivered loose from the words like dust falling from old pipes:

Soon, soon, the momma bird sings.
Take flight, take flight!

Part of an old nursery rhyme. *Beat your wings,* Mission whispered, remembering the rest, a story about a young crow learning to be free. *Beat your wings and fly away to brighter things. Fly, fly with all your might!* He started to check the back for a real note, something beyond this fragment of a rhyme, when someone banged on the window again. Several of the other boys dropped their charcoals and visibly startled. One boy cursed under his breath. Mission whirled around to see Jeffery on the other side of the glass, a covered meal tray balanced on one palm, his bald head jerking impatiently.

Mission folded the letter up and stuffed it back in the envelope. He raised his hand over his head to let Jeffery know he'd be right there, licked one finger and ran it across the sticky paste, re-sealing the envelope as best he could. "Good luck," he told Bradley, even though he had no clue what the kid thought he was doing. He dragged his pack off the table, was careful to wipe away the chalk dust that had spilled, and hurried out of the conference room.

"Let's go," Jeffery said, clearly annoyed.

Mission hurried after him. He glanced back once at the window, then over at the noisy crowd jostling against the temporary barriers by the door. An IT tech approached the crowd with a computer, wires coiled neatly on top, and a woman reached out desperate arms from behind the barrier like a mother yearning for her baby.

"Since when did people start bringing their own computers up?" he asked, curious as a seasoned porter about how things got from there to here and back again. It felt as though he were witnessing yet another loop his kind was being sliced out of. Roker would have a fit.

"Yesterday. Mr. Wyck stopped sending our techs out. He says it's safer this way. People being robbed out there and not enough security to go around."

Jeffery was waved through the gates, Mission as well. They wound in silence through the hallways, every office full of clacking sounds or people arguing. Mission saw electrical parts and paper strewn everywhere. He wondered which office was Rodny's and why nobody else was having their food delivered. Maybe his friend was in trouble. That was it. Made sense of everything. Maybe he had pulled one of his stunts. Did they have a holding cell on thirty-four? He didn't think so. He was about to ask Jeffery if Rodny was in the pen when the old security guard stopped at an imposing steel door.

"Here." He held the tray out to Mission, who stuck the letter between his lips and accepted it. Jeffery glanced back, blocked Mission's view of a keypad with his body, and tapped in a code. A series of clunks sounded in the jamb of the heavy door. Fucking right, Rodny was in trouble. What kind of pen was this?

The door swung inward. Jeffery grabbed the tray and told Mission to wait there. Mission still had the taste of milk paste on his lips as he watched the security chief step inside a room that seemed to go back quite a ways. The lights inside pulsed as if something was wrong, red warning lights like a fire alarm. Jeffery called out for Rodny while Mission tried to peek around the guard for a better look.

Rodny arrived a moment later, almost as if expecting them. His eyes widened when he saw Mission standing there. Mission fought to close his own mouth, which he could feel hanging open at the sight of his friend.

"Hey." Rodny opened the heavy door a little further and glanced down the hallway. "What're you doing here?"

"Good to see you, too," Mission said. He held out the letter. "The Crow sent this."

"Ah, official business." Rodny smiled. "You're here as a porter, eh? Not a friend?"

Rodny smiled, but Mission could see that his friend was beat. He looked like he hadn't slept for days. His hair had been chopped short as if to keep it out of the way, but there was the shadow of a beard on his chin. Mission glanced into the room, wondering what they had him doing in there. Tall black metal cabinets were all he could see. They stretched out of sight, neatly spaced.

"You learning to fix refrigerators?" Mission asked.

Rodny glanced over his shoulder. He laughed. "Those are computers." He still had that tone like one who thought himself older or better. Mission nearly reminded his friend that today was his birthday, that they were the same age. Rodny was the only one he ever felt like reminding. Jeffery cleared his throat impatiently, seemed annoyed by the chatter.

Rodny turned to the security chief. "You mind if we have a few seconds?" he asked.

Jeffery shifted his weight, the stiff leather of his boots squeaking. "You know I can't," he said. "I'll probably get chewed out for allowing even this."

"You're right." Rodny shook his head like he shouldn't have asked. Mission studied the exchange. He sensed that his friend was the same one he'd ever known. He was in trouble for something, probably being forced to do the most reviled task in all of IT for a brash thing he'd said or done. He smiled at the thought.

Rodny tensed suddenly as though he'd heard something deep inside the room. He held up a finger to the others and asked them to wait there. "Just a second," he said, rushing off, bare feet slapping on the steel floors.

Jeffery crossed his arms and looked Mission up and down unhappily. "You two grow up down the hall from each other?"

"Went to school together," Mission said. "So what did Rod do? You know, Mrs. Crowe used to make us sweep the entire Nest and clean the blackboards if we cut up in class. We did our fair share of sweeping, the two of us."

Jeffery appraised him for a moment. And then his expressionless face shattered into tooth and grin. "You think your friend is in trouble," he said. He seemed on the verge of laughing. "Son, you have no idea."

Before Mission could inquire, Rodny returned, smiling and breathless.

"Sorry," he said to Jeffery. "I had to get that." He turned to Mission. "Thanks for coming by, man. Good to see you."

That was it?

"Good to see you, too," Mission sputtered, surprised that their visit would be so brief. "Hey, don't be a stranger." He went to give his old friend a hug, but Rodny stuck out a hand instead. Mission looked at it for a pause, confused, wondering if they'd grown apart so far so fast.

"Give my best to everyone," Rodny said, as if he might never see them again himself.

Jeffery cleared his throat, clearly annoyed and ready to go.

"I will," Mission said, fighting to keep the sadness out of his voice. He accepted his friend's hand. They shook like strangers, the smile on Rodny's face quivering, the folds of the note hidden in his palm digging sharply into Mission's hand.

·12·

I t was a miracle Mission didn't drop the note as it was passed to him, a miracle that he knew something was amiss, to keep his mouth closed, to not stand there a fool in front of Jeffery and say, "Hey, what's this?" Instead, he kept the wad of paper balled in his fist as he was escorted back toward the security station. They were nearly there when someone called "Porter!" from one of the offices they passed.

Jeffery placed a hand on Mission's chest, forcing him to a stop. They turned, and a familiar man strode down the hallway to meet them. It was Mr. Wyck, Head of IT, familiar to most porters. The endless shuffle of broken and repaired computers once kept the Upper Dispatch as busy as Supply kept the lower. Mission gathered that may have changed since yesterday.

"You on duty, son?" Mr. Wyck studied the porter's 'chief knotted around Mission's neck.

"Yessir." Mission hid the note from Rodny behind his back. He pressed it into his pocket with his thumb, like a seed going to soil. "You need something moved, sir?"

"I do." Mr. Wyck studied him for a moment. "You're the Jones boy, right? The zero."

Mission felt a flash of heat around his neck at the use of the term, a reference to the fact that no lottery number had been pulled for him. "Yessir. It's Mission." He offered his hand. Mr. Wyck accepted it.

"Yes, yes. I went to school with your father. And your mother, of course."

He paused to give Mission time to respond. Mission ground his teeth together and said nothing. He let go of the man's hand before his sweaty palms had a chance to speak for him.

"Say I wanted to move something without going through Dispatch." Mr. Wyck smiled. "And say I wanted to avoid the sort of nastiness that took place last night a few levels up from here."

Mission glanced over at Jeffery, who seemed disinterested in the conversation. It was strange to hear this sort of offer from a man of authority in front of a member of Security, but there was one thing Mission had discovered since he emerged from his shadowing days: things only got darker.

"I don't follow," Mission said. He fought the urge to turn and see how far they were from the security gate. A woman emerged from an office down the hall, behind Mr. Wyck. Jeffery made a gesture with his hand, and she stopped and kept her distance, out of earshot.

"I think you do, and I admire your discretion," Mr. Wyck said. "Two hundred chits to move a package a half dozen levels from Supply."

Mission tried to remain calm. Two hundred chits. A month's pay for half a day's work. But he feared this was some sort of test. Maybe Rodny had gotten in trouble for flunking a similar one.

"I don't know—" he said.

"It's an open invite," Wyck said. "The next porter that comes through will get the same offer. I don't care who does it, but the first will get the chits. You don't have to answer me. Just show up and ask for Joyce at the Supply counter. Tell her you're doing a job for Wyck. There'll be a delivery report detailing the rest."

"I'll think about it, sir."

"Good." Mr. Wyck smiled.

"Anything else?"

"No, no. You're free to go." He nodded to Jeffery, who snapped back from wherever he'd checked out to.

"Thank you, sir." Mission turned and followed the chief.

"Oh, and happy birthday, son," Mr. Wyck called out.

Mission glanced back, didn't say thanks, just hurried after Jeffery and through the security gate, past the crowds and out on the landing, down two turns of stairs, where he finally reached into his pocket for the note from Rodny. Paranoid he might drop it and watch it bounce off the stairs and through the rail, he gingerly and methodically unfolded the scrap of paper. It looked like the same rag blend Mrs. Crowe's note had been written on, the same threads of purple and red mixed in with the rough gray weave. For a moment, Mission feared the note would be addressed to the Crow rather than to him, maybe more lines in old nursery rhymes. He worked the piece of paper flat, one side blank, turned it over to read the other.

It wasn't addressed to anyone. Just two words, and Mission remembered the way his friend's smile had quivered while they shook hands.

Mission felt suddenly alone. There was the smell of something burning lingering in the stairwell, a tinge of smoke that mixed with the paint from drying graffiti. He took the small note and tore it into ever smaller pieces. He kept tearing until there was nothing left to pinch with his fingers, nothing left to shred. He waited until a passing man spiraled out of sight and then sprinkled the dull confetti over the rail to drift down and disappear into the void.

The evidence was gone, but the message lingered vividly in his mind. The hasty scrawl, the shadowy scratch the edge of a coin or a spoon made as it was dragged across paper, two words barely legible from his friend who never needed anybody or asked for anything:

Help me.

And that was all.

• Silo 1 •

Time is too slow for those who wait,
too swift for those who fear,
too long for those who grieve,
too short for those who rejoice,
but for those who love, time is eternity.

-Henry Van Dyke

·13·

Finding the right silo was easy enough. Donald could look at the old schematic and remember standing on those hills, peering down into the wide bowls that held each facility. The sound of grumbling four-wheelers came back, the plumes of dust kicked up as they bounced across the ridges where the grass had not yet filled in. He remembered that they had been growing grass over those hills, straw and seed spread everywhere, a bit of an illusion, a task hindsight made both pointless and sad.

Standing on that ridge in his memory, he was able to picture the Tennessee delegation. It would be Silo 2. Once he had this, he dug deeper. It took a bit of fumbling to remember how the computer program worked, how to sift through lives that lived in databases. There was an entire history there of each silo if you knew how to read it, all those souls trapped in little cells, but the history only went so far. It went back to made-up names, back to the orientation. It didn't stretch to the Legacy beyond. The old world was hidden behind bombs and a fog of mist and forgetting.

He had the right silo, but locating Helen might prove impossible. He worked frantically while Anna sang in the shower.

She had left the bathroom door open, steam and her melodic humming both billowing out. Donald ignored what he took to be an invitation. He ignored the throbbing, the yearning, the hormonal rush of being near an ex-lover after centuries of need. He searched instead for his wife.

There were four thousand names in that first generation of Silo 2. Four thousand, exactly. Roughly half were female. There were three Helens. Each had a grainy picture taken for her work ID stored on the servers. None of the Helens matched what he remembered his wife looking like, what he *thought* she looked like. Tears came unbidden. He wiped them away, furious at himself. From the shower, Anna sang a sad lament from long ago while Donald flipped through random photos. After a dozen, the faces of strangers began to meld together and threaten to erode the Helen in his memory. He went back to searching by name. Surely he could guess the name she would've chosen. He had picked Troy for himself those many years ago, a clue leading him back to her. He liked to think she would've done the same.

He tried Sandra, her mother's name, but neither of the two hits were right. He tried Danielle, her sister's name. One hit. Not her.

She wouldn't come up with something random, would she? They had talked once of what they might name their kids. It was gods and goddesses, a joke at first, but Helen had fallen in love with the name Athena. He did a search. Zero hits in that first generation.

The pipes squealed as Anna turned off the shower. Her singing subsided back into a hum, a song of sadness and grief, a hymn for the funeral they were about to attend. Donald tried a few more names, anxious to discover something, anything. He would search every night while the silo slept if he had to. He would search while he pretended to work on this problem with the silos. He wouldn't sleep until he knew, until he found her.

"Do you need to shower before the service?" Anna called out from the bathroom.

He didn't want to go to the service, he nearly said. He knew Victor as someone to fear, a boss sitting across the hallway, always watching, dispensing drugs, manipulating him. At least, that's how the paranoia of those days made it all seem.

"I'll go like this," he said. He still wore the beige coveralls they'd given him the day before. He flipped through random pictures again, starting at the top of the alphabet. What other name? The fear was that he'd forget what she looked like. Or that she'd look more and more like Anna in his mind. He couldn't let that happen.

"Find anything?"

She snuck up behind him and reached for something on the desk. A towel was wrapped around her breasts and reached the middle of her thighs. Her skin was wet. She grabbed a hairbrush and walked, humming, back to the bathroom. Donald forgot to answer. His body responded to Anna in a way that made him furious and full of guilt. The monitor fogged from the steam. He felt clammy from something else.

He was still married, he reminded himself. He would be until he knew what'd happened to Helen. He would be loyal to her forever.

Loyalty.

On a whim, he searched for the name Karma.

One hit. Donald sat up straight. His palms felt damp. He hadn't imagined a hit. It was their dog's name, the nearest thing he and Helen ever had to a child of their own. He brought up the picture.

"I guess we're all wearing these horrid outfits to the funeral, right?" Anna passed the desk as she snapped up the front of her white coveralls. Donald only noticed in the corner of his tear-filled vision. He covered his mouth and felt his body tremble with suppressed sobs. On the monitor, in a tiny square of black and white pixels in the middle of a work badge, was his wife.

"You'll be ready to go in a few minutes, won't you?"

Anna disappeared back into the bathroom, brushing her hair. Donald wiped his cheeks, salt on his lips while he read. Anna's humming made it nearly impossible.

Karma Brewer. There were several occupations listed, with a badge photo for each. Teacher, School Master, Judge—more wrinkles in each picture but always the same half-smile. He opened the full file, thinking suddenly what it would've been like to have been on the very first shift in Silo 1, to watch her life unfold next door, maybe even reach out and contact her somehow. A judge. It'd been a dream of hers to be a judge one day. Donald wept while Anna hummed. Through a lens of tears, he read about his wife.

Married, it said, which didn't throw up any flags at first. Married, of course. To him. Until he read about her death. Eighty-two years old. Survived by Rick Brewer and two children, Athena and Mars.

Rick Brewer.

The walls and ceiling bulged inward. Donald felt a chill, the cold of the pod and the deep sleep returning to his veins. There were more pictures. He followed the links to other files. To this husband's files.

"Mick," Anna whispered behind him.

Donald startled and turned to find her reading over his shoulder. Drying tears streaked his face, but he didn't care. His best friend and his wife. Two kids. He turned back to the screen and pulled up the daughter's file. Athena's. There were several pictures from different careers and phases of her life. She had Helen's mouth.

"Donny. Please don't."

A hand on his shoulder. Donald flinched from it and watched an animation wrought by furious clicks, this child growing into an approximation of his wife, until the girl's own children appeared in her file.

"Donny," Anna whispered. "We're gonna be late for the funeral."

Donald wept. Sobs tore through him as if he were made of tissue. "Late," he cried. "A hundred years too late." He sputtered this last, overcome with misery. There was a granddaughter on the screen that was not his, a great granddaughter one more click away. They stared out at him, all of them, none with eyes like his own.

·14·

Donald went to Victor's funeral numb. He rode the elevator in silence, watched his boots kick ahead of himself as he teetered forward, but what he found on the medical level wasn't a funeral at all—it was body disposal. It was them storing the remains back in a pod because they had no dirt in which to bury their dead. Their food came from cans. Their bodies returned to the same.

Donald was introduced to Erskine, who explained unprompted that the body would not rot. The same invisible machines that allowed them to survive the freezing process and turned their waking piss the color of charcoal would keep the dead as soft and fresh as the living. Donald heard all of this. He watched as the man he had known as Victor was prepped for deep freeze. As a reflex, he looked for something on a clipboard to sign, some nominal gesture that he was in charge, that anyone there was in charge.

They wheeled the body down a hall and through a sea of pods. The deep freeze was a cemetery, Donald saw. A grid of bodies laid flat, only a name to feebly encapsulate all that lay within. He wondered how many of the pods contained the dead. Some men must die on their shifts from natural causes. Some must break down as Victor had. They weren't immortal, he and these people, they were simply skipping through time. And some of those skipping undoubtedly stumbled and fell.

Donald helped with the physical task of moving the body into the pod. There were only four of them present, only four who could know how Victor had gone. The illusion that someone was in charge must be maintained. Donald thought of his last job, sitting at a desk, hands on a rudderless wheel, pretending. He watched Thurman as the old man kissed his palm and pressed his fingers to Victor's cheek. The lid was closed. The cold of the room made their exhalations visible, a funeral on a crisp fall day.

The others took turns speaking, but it was Helen's funeral that Donald attended. He did not cry. He had sobbed on the elevator, Anna holding him. Now, it was only the shock and the long years between. He did the math. Helen had died almost a century ago. It had been longer than that since he'd lost her over that hill, since missing her messages, since not being able to get through to her. He remembered the national anthem and the bombs filling the air. He remembered his sister being there.

His sister.

It was more than a century since those bombs had gone off, but that girl who had sung the national anthem would be stored in one of these cavernous rooms. Donald's sister would be there as well. Family. There was a fierce urge to find her and wake her, to bring someone he loved back to life. He wanted to hold a loved one while the last of the cold thawed from their veins.

Dr. Erskine paid his final respects. Only four of them present to mourn this man who had killed billions. Donald felt Anna's presence beside him and wondered if maybe the lack of a crowd was in fact due to her. Here were the four who knew not only that a man had taken his life, but that a woman had been woken. Her father knew, Dr. Henson, who had performed the procedure, Erskine, whom she spoke of as a friend, and himself.

The absurdity of Donald's existence, of the state of the world, swooped down on him in that gathering. He did not belong. He was only there because of a girl he had dated in college, a girl whose father was a senator, whose affections had likely gotten him elected, who had dragged him into a murderous scheme, and had now pulled him from a frozen death. All the great coincidences and marvelous achievements of his life disappeared in a flash. In their place were puppet strings. He was a pawn being shoved around a board while marveling at his great adventure. There was no coincidence at all, nothing to be amazed by, just dangerous affections.

"A tragic loss, this."

Donald emerged from his ruminations to discover that the ceremony was over. Anna and her father stood two rows of pods away discussing something. Dr. Henson was down by the base of the pod, the panel beeping as he made adjustments. That left Donald with Dr. Erskine, a thin man with glasses and a British accent. He surveyed Donald from the opposite side of the pod. Donald had been introduced to him earlier as he stepped off the elevator, but he'd been in a mournful haze.

"He was on my shift," Donald said inanely, trying to explain why he was present for the service. There was little else he could think to say of this man whom he had known as Victor. He stepped closer and peered through the little window at the calm face within.

"I know," Erskine said. This wiry man, probably in his early to mid sixties, adjusted the glasses on his narrow nose and joined Donald in peering through the small window. "He was quite fond of you, you know."

"I didn't," Donald blurted out, unable to censor himself. "I mean . . . he never said as much to me."

"He was peculiar that way." Erskine studied the deceased with a smile. "Brilliant perhaps for knowing the minds of others, just not so keen on communicating with them."

Donald studied this Dr. Erskine. He tried to remember what little Anna had told him about the man. "Did you know him from before?" he asked. He wasn't sure how else to broach the subject. The *before* seemed taboo with some, freely spoken of by others.

Erskine nodded. "We worked together. Well, in the same hospital. We orbited each other for quite a few years until my . . . discovery." He reached out and touched the glass, a final farewell to an old friend, it seemed.

"What discovery?" He vaguely remembered Anna mentioning something.

Erskine glanced up. Looking closer, Donald thought he may have been in his seventies. It was hard to tell. He had some of the agelessness of Thurman, like an antique that patinas and will grow no older.

"I'm the one who discovered the great threat," he said. It sounded more an admission of guilt than a proud claim. It was said with sadness. At the base of the pod, Dr. Henson finished his adjustments, stood, and excused himself. He steered the empty gurney toward the exit.

"The nanos." Donald remembered; Anna had said as much. He watched Thurman debate something with his daughter, his fist coming down over and over into his palm, and a question came to mind. He wanted to hear it from someone else. He wanted to see if the lies matched, if that meant they might be the truth.

"You were a medical doctor?" he asked.

Erskine considered the question. It seemed a simple enough one to answer.

"Not precisely," he said, his accent thick. "I *built* medical doctors. Wee ones." He pinched the air and squinted through his glasses at his own fingers. "We were working on ways to keep soldiers safe. Until I found someone else's handiwork in a sample of blood. It wasn't long before I was finding the little bastards everywhere."

Anna and Thurman headed their way, Anna with her cap donned once more, her hair in a bun that bulged noticeably through the top. It was little disguise for what she was, useful perhaps at a distance.

"I'd like to ask you about that sometime," Donald said hurriedly. "It might help my . . . help me with this problem the silos are having."

"Of course," Erskine said. His accent made him sound cheerier than he appeared.

"I need to get back," Anna told Donald. She set her lips in a thin grimace, like a scar on her face, a wound from the argument with her father, and Donald finally appreciated how powerless and trapped she truly was. He imagined a year spent in that warehouse of war, clues scattered across that planning table, sleeping on that small cot, not able even to ride up to the cafeteria to see the hills and the dark clouds or have a meal at the time of her own choosing, relying on others to bring her everything.

"I'll escort the young man up," Donald heard Erskine say, his hand resting on Donald's shoulder. "I'd like to chat with our boy for a bit."

Thurman narrowed his eyes but relented. Anna squeezed Donald's hand a final time, glanced at the humming pod, and headed toward the exit. Her father followed a few quiet paces behind.

"Come with me." Erskine's breath fogged the air. "I want to show you someone."

They left the cooling pod, and now it was just one of many. Identical. There were no flowers to mark what had happened, no mound of moist soil standing out like a brown scab on green grass. There was simply a lid closed on a life, no different from so many others. And a name. A made-up and pointless name.

·15·

Erskine picked his way through the grid of pods with purpose as though he'd walked the route dozens of times. Donald followed after, rubbing his arms for warmth. He had been too long in that crypt-like place. The cold was leeching back into his flesh.

"Thurman keeps saying we were already dead," he told Erskine, attacking the question head-on. "Is that true?"

Erskine looked back over his shoulder. He waited for Donald to catch up, seemed to consider this question.

"Well," Donald asked. "Were we?"

"I never saw a design with a hundred percent efficiency," Erskine said. "We weren't there with our own work, and theirs was much cruder. But what they had already would've taken out most. That part's true enough." He resumed his walk through the field of sleeping corpses. "Even the most severe epidemics burn themselves out," he said, "so it's difficult to say. I argued for countermeasures. Victor argued for this." He spread his arms over the quiet assembly.

"And Victor won."

"Indeed."

"Do you think he . . . had second thoughts? Is that why . . . ?"

Erskine stopped at one of the pods and placed both hands on its icy surface. "I'm sure we all have second thoughts," he said sadly. "But I don't think Vic ever doubted the rightness of this mission. I don't know why he did what he did in the end. It wasn't like him."

Donald peered inside the pod Erskine had led him to. There was a middle-aged woman inside, her eyelids covered in frost.

"My daughter," Erskine said. "My only child."

There was a moment of silence. It allowed the faint hum of a thousand pods to be heard. It could've been a choir of monks making that sound, a quiet hum on so many closed lips.

"When Thurman made the decision to wake his Anna, all I could dream about was doing the same. But why? There was no reason, no need for her expertise. Caroline was an accountant. And besides, it wouldn't be fair to drag her from her dreams."

Donald wanted to ask if it would ever be fair. What world did Erskine expect his daughter to ever see again? When would she wake to a normal life? A pleasant life?

"When I found nanos in her blood, I knew this was the right thing to do." He turned to Donald. "I know you're looking for answers, son. We all are. This is a cruel world. It's always been a cruel world. I spent my whole life looking for ways to make it better, to patch things up, dreaming of an ideal. But for every sot like me, there's ten more out there getting their jollies trying to tear things down. And it only takes one of them to get lucky."

Donald flashed back to the day Thurman had given him The Order. That thick book was the start of his plummet into madness. He remembered their talk in that massive lozenge of a medical unit, the feeling of being infected, the paranoia that something harmful and invisible was invading him. But if Erskine and Thurman were telling the truth, he'd been infected long before that.

"You weren't poisoning me that day." He looked from the pod to Erskine, piecing something together. "The interview with Thurman, the weeks and weeks he spent in that chamber having all of those meetings. You weren't infecting us."

Erskine nodded ever so slightly. "We were healing you," he said.

Donald felt a sudden flash of anger. "Then why not heal *everyone?*" he demanded.

"We discussed that. I had the same thought. To me, it was an engineering problem. I wanted to build countermeasures, machines to kill machines before they got to us. Thurman had similar ideas. He saw it as an invisible war, one we desperately needed to take to the enemy. We all saw the battles we were accustomed to fighting, you see. Me in the bloodstream, Thurman overseas. It was Victor who set the two of us straight."

Erskine pulled a cloth from his breast pocket and removed his glasses. He rubbed them while he talked, his voice echoing in whispers from the walls. "Victor said there would be no end to it. He pointed to computer viruses to make his case, how one might run rampant and cripple hundreds of millions of machines. Sooner or later, some nano attack would get through, get out of control, and there would be an epidemic built on bits of code rather than strands of DNA."

"So what?" Donald asked. "We've dealt with plagues before. Why would this be different?" He swept his arms at the pods. "Tell me how the solution isn't worse than the problem?"

As worked up as he felt, he also sensed how much angrier he would be if he heard this from Thurman. He wondered if he'd been set up to have a kindlier man, a stranger, take him aside and tell him what Thurman thought he needed to hear. It was hard not to be paranoid about being manipulated, to not feel the strings still knotted to his joints.

"Psychology," Erskine replied. He put his glasses back on. "This is where Victor set us straight, why our ideas would never work. I'll never forget the conversation. We were sitting in the cafeteria at Walter Reed. Thurman was there to hand out ribbons, but really to meet with the two of us." He shook his head. "It was crowded in there. If anyone knew the things we were discussing . . ."

"Psychology," Donald reminded him. "Tell me how this is better. *More* people die this way."

Erskine snapped back to the present. "That's where we were wrong, just like you. Imagine the first discovery that one of these epidemics was man-made—the panic, the violence that would ensue. That's where the end would come. A typhoon kills a few hundred people, does a few billion in damage, and what do we do?" Erskine interlocked his fingers. "We come together. We put the pieces back. But a terrorist's bomb." He frowned. "A terrorist's bomb does the same damage, and it throws the world into turmoil."

He spread his hands apart like an explosion going off.

"When there's only God to blame, we forgive him. When it's our fellow man, we must destroy him."

Donald shook his head. He didn't know what to believe. But then he thought about the fear and rage he'd felt when he thought he'd been infected by something in that chamber. Meanwhile, he never worried about the billions of creatures swimming in his gut and doing so since the day he was born.

"We can't tweak the genes of the food we eat without suspicion," Erskine added. "We can pick and choose the naturally mutated ones until a blade of grass is a great ear of corn, but we can't do it with *purpose*. Vic had dozens of examples like these. He rattled them off in the cafeteria that day." Erskine ticked his fingers as he counted. "Vaccines versus natural immunities, cloning versus twins, modified foods. Or course he was perfectly right. The bastard always was. It was the manmade part that would have caused the chaos. It would be knowing that people were out to get us, that there was danger in the air we breathed."

Erskine paused for a moment. Donald's mind was racing.

"You know, Vic once said that if these terrorists had an ounce of sense, they would've simply announced what they were working on and then sat back to watch things burn on their own. He said that's all it would take, us knowing that it was happening, that the end of any of us could come silent, invisible, and any damn time."

"And so the solution was to burn it all to the ground *ourselves?*" Donald ran his hands through his hair, trying to make sense of it all. His teeth began to clatter. He thought of a firefighting technique that always seemed just as confusing to him, the burning of wide swaths of forest to prevent a fire from spreading. And he knew in Iran, when oil wells were set ablaze during the first war, that sometimes the only cure was to set off a bomb, to fight the inferno with something greater.

"Believe me," Erskine said, "I came up with my own complaints. Endless complaints. But I knew the truth from the beginning, it just took me a while to accept it. Thurman was won over more easily. He saw at once that we needed to get off this ball of rock, to start over. But the cost of travel was too great."

"Why travel through space?" Donald said, "when you can travel through time?" He remembered a conversation in Thurman's office about making room on this planet rather than going off in search of another. The old man had told him what he was planning that very first day.

Erskine's eyes widened. "Yes. That was his argument. He'd seen enough war, I suppose. Me, I didn't have Thurman's experiences or the professional . . . *distance* Vic enjoyed. It was the analogy of the computer virus that wore me down, seeing these nanos like a new cyber war. I knew what they could do, how fast they could restructure themselves, evolve, if you will. We could've gone back and forth for ages, but there would've been no end to it. Once it started, it would only stop when we were no longer around. And maybe not even then. Every defense would become a blueprint for the next attack. The air would choke with our invisible armies. There would be great clouds of them, mutating and fighting without need of a host. And once the public saw this and *knew* . . ." he left the sentence unfinished.

"Hysteria," Donald muttered.

"Hysteria and homebrew. If you think affordable DNA sequencers were a scare, or those cloning kits that made the rounds, imagine kids programming nanos in their basements, sharing their designs on the web. It would be worse than when they started printing those plastic guns in those cheap extruder kits. Who knows what they might try and target just for fun? It starts with the neighbor's cat. The next weekend, someone wipes out an entire species by accident."

"You said it might not ever end, even if we were gone. Does that mean they're still out there? The nanos?"

Erskine glanced toward the ceiling. "The world outside isn't just being scrubbed of humans right now, if that's what you're asking.

It's being reset. All of our experiments are being removed. By the grace of God, it'll be a very long time indeed before we think to perform them again."

Donald remembered from orientation that the combined shifts would last five hundred years. Half a millennia of living underground. How much scrubbing was necessary? And what was to keep them from heading down that same path a second time? How would any of them unlearn the potential dangers? You don't get the fire back in the box once you've unleashed it.

"You asked me if Victor had regrets—" Erskine coughed into his fist and nodded. "I do think he felt something close to that once. It was something he said to me as he was coming off his eighth or ninth shift, I don't remember which. I think I was heading into my sixth. This was just after the two of you worked together, after that nasty business with Silo 12—"

"My first shift," Donald said, since Erskine seemed to be counting. He wanted to add that it was his only shift. It was his final shift.

"Yes, of course." Erskine adjusted his glasses. "I'm sure you knew him well enough to know that he didn't show his emotions often."

"He was difficult to read," Donald agreed. He knew almost nothing of the man he had just helped to bury.

"So you'll appreciate this, I think. We were riding the lift together, and Vic turns to me and says how hard it is to sit there at that desk of his and see what we were doing to the men across the hall. He meant you, of course. People in your position."

Donald tried to imagine the man he knew saying such a thing. He wanted to believe it.

"But that's not what really struck me. I've never seen him sadder than when he said the following. He said—" Erskine rested a hand on the pod. "He said that sitting there, watching you people work at your desks, getting to know you—he often thought that the world would be a better place with people like you in charge."

"People like me?" Donald shook his head. "What does that even mean?"

Erskine smiled. "I asked him precisely that. His response was that it was a burden doing what he knew to be correct, to be sound and logical." Erskine ran one hand across the pod as if he could touch his daughter within. "And how much simpler things would be, how much better for us all, if we had people brave enough to do what was *right*, instead."

·16·

I t was that night that Anna came to him. After a day of numbness and dwelling on death, of eating the meals brought down by Thurman and not tasting a bite, of watching her set up a computer for him and spread out folders of notes, she came to him in the darkness.

Donald complained. He tried to push her away. She sat on the edge of the cot and held his wrists while he sobbed and grew feeble. He thought of Erskine's story, on what it meant to do the right thing rather than the correct thing, what the difference was. He thought this as an old lover draped herself across him, her hand on the back of his neck, her cheek on his shoulder, lying there against him while he wept.

A century of sleep had weakened him, he thought. A century of sleep and the knowledge that Mick and Helen had lived a life together. He felt suddenly angry at her. Not at Anna, whose breath he could feel on his neck, but at Helen. Angry at her for not holding out, for not living alone, for not getting his messages and meeting him over the hill where he could store her beauty away forever.

Anna kissed his cheek and whispered that everything would be okay. Fresh tears flowed down Donald's face as he realized that he was everything Victor had assumed he wasn't. He was a miserable human being for wishing his wife to be lonely so that he could sleep at night a hundred years later. He was a miserable human being for denying her that solace when Anna's touch made him feel so much better.

"I can't," he whispered for the dozenth time.

"Shhh," Anna said. She brushed his hair back in the darkness. And the two of them were alone in that room where wars were waged. They were trapped together with those crates of arms, with guns and ammo, and far more dangerous things.

• Silo 18 •

Do not let me fear my death.
I beg you with my final breath.
Take and plant me 'neath the corn.
Take me, oh Lord, another born.
One for one, as per your plan.
One for one, come take my hand.
Bury me that I'll take root.
Plant me, oh Lord, and reap your fruit.

-Seth Hayden, age 5

·17·

Mission wound his way toward Central Dispatch and agonized over what to do for his friend. He felt afraid for Rodny but powerless to help. The door they had him behind was unlike any he'd ever seen: thick and solid, gleaming and daunting. If the trouble his friend had caused could be read by where they were keeping him—

He shuddered to continue that line of thought. It'd only been a few months since the last cleaning. Mission had been there, had carried up part of the suit, a more haunting experience than porting a body for burial. Dead bodies at least were placed in those black bags the coroners used. There was something good and somber about them. The cleaning suit was a different sort of bag, tailored to a living soul that would crawl inside and be forced to die there.

Mission remembered where they had picked up the gear. It'd been a room right down the hall from where Rodny was being kept. Weren't cleanings run by the same department? He shivered. One slip of a tongue could land a body out there, rotting on the hills, and his friend Rodny was known to wag his dangerously.

First his mother, and now his best friend. Mission wondered what the Pact said about volunteering to clean in one's stead. If it said anything at all. Amazing that he could live under the rules of a document that he'd never read. He just assumed others had, all the people in charge, and that they were operating by its contents fairly.

On fifty-eight, a porter's 'chief tied to the downbound railing caught his attention. It was the same blue pattern as the 'chief worn around his neck, but with a bright red merchant's hem. Duty beckoned, dispelling thoughts that were spiraling nowhere. Mission unknotted the 'chief and searched the fabric for the merchant's stamp. It was Drexel's, the apothecary down the hall. Light loads and lighter pay, normally. But at least it was downbound, unless Drexel had been careless again with which rail he tied it to.

Mission was dying to get to Central where a shower and a change of clothes awaited, but if anyone spotted him with a flat pack marching past a signal 'chief, he'd hear it from Morgan and the others. He hurried inside to Drexel's, praying it wasn't a round of meds going to several dozen individual apartments. His legs turned to rubber just thinking about it.

Drexel was at the counter as Mission pushed open the apothecary's squeaky door. A large man with a full beard and a balding head, Drexel was something of a fixture in the mids. Many came to him rather than to the doctors, though Mission wasn't sure how sound a choice that was. Often, though, it was the man with the most promises who got the chits, not the one who made people better. And besides, the very worst cases rarely complained. If they did, only the roots heard.

The usual handful of sick people sat on Drexel's benches in the waiting room, sniffling and coughing. Mission felt the urge to cover his mouth with his 'chief. Instead, he innocuously held his breath and waited while Drexel filled a small square of paper with ground powder, folding it neatly like one might roll a cigarette, before handing it to the woman waiting. The woman slid a few chits across the counter. When she walked away, Mission tossed the signal 'chief on top of the money.

"Ah, Mish. Good to see you, boy. Looking fit as a fiddle." Drexel smoothed his beard and smiled, yellow teeth peering out from cornrows of drooping whiskers.

"Same," Mission said politely, braving a breath. "Got something for me?"

"I do. One sec."

Drexel disappeared behind a wall of shelves crammed full of tiny vials and jars. A baby in the waiting room wailed. The apothecary reappeared with a small sack. "Meds for down below," he said.

"I can take them as far as Central and have Dispatch send them from there," Mission told him. "I'm just finishing up a shift."

Drexel frowned and rubbed his beard. "I suppose that'll do. And Dispatch'll bill me?"

Mission held out a palm. "If you tip," he said.

"Aye, a tip. But only if you solve a riddle." Drexel leaned on the counter, which seemed to sag beneath his bulk. The snifflers and coughers waiting on their meds were ignored, and the last thing Mission wanted to hear was another of the old man's riddles and then not get paid. Always an excuse with Drexel to keep a chit on his side of the counter.

"Okay," the apothecary began, tugging on his whiskers. "Which one weighs more, a bag full of seventy-eight pounds of feathers, or a bag full of seventy-eight pounds of rocks?"

Mission didn't hesitate with his answer. "The bag of feathers," he declared. He'd heard this one before. It was a riddle made for a porter, and he had thought on it long enough between the levels to come up with his own answer, one different from the obvious.

"Incorrect!" Drexel roared, waving a finger. "It isn't the rocks—" His face dimmed. "Wait. Did you say the feathers?" He shook his head. "No, boy, they weigh the *same*."

"The contents weigh the same," Mission told him. "The bag of feathers would have to be bigger. You said they were both full, which means a bigger bag with more material, and so it weighs more." He held out his palm. Drexel stood there, chewing his beard for a moment, thrown off his game. Begrudgingly, he took two coins from the lady's pay and placed them in Mission's hand. Mission accepted them and stuffed the sack of meds into his pack before cinching it up tight.

"The bigger bag—" Drexel muttered, as Mission hurried off, past the benches, holding his breath again as he went, the pills rattling in his sack.

The apothecary's annoyance was worth far more than the tip, but Mission appreciated both. The enjoyment faded, however, as he spiraled down through a tense silo. There was a fear invisible but still sensed like the rising smoke. He saw deputies on one landing, hands on their guns, trying to calm down fighting neighbors. The glass on the windows peeking into a shop on forty-two were broken and covered with a sheet of plastic. Mission was pretty sure that was recent. And down he went, the stairway trembling, the graffiti on the walls warning him with grammatical troubles of what was yet to come.

He arrived at Central Dispatch to find it eerily quiet. Marko passed him in the hall. The older porter had a black eye, and

Mission had a good idea of where it came from. He nodded, and Marko nodded back, a bit of respect from a veteran porter who had warred with him in the dark the night before. Mission felt sad for the things he could imagine doing for a little respect. Braving violence was an ignoble way to earn it.

He made his way past the sorting rooms with their tall shelves of items needing delivery and went straight to the main counter. He would drop off his current package and pick out his next job before changing and showering. Katelyn was working the counter. There were no other porters queued up. Off licking their wounds, perhaps. Or maybe seeing to their families during this recent spate of violence.

"Hey, Katelyn."

"Mish." She smiled. "You look intact."

He laughed and touched his nose, which was still sore. "Thanks."

"Cam just passed through asking where you were."

"Yeah?" Mission was surprised. He figured his friend would be taking a day off with the bonus from the coroner. "Did he pick something up?"

"Yup. He requested anything heading toward Supply. Was in a better mood than usual, though he seemed miffed to have been left out of last night's adventures."

"He heard about that, huh?" Mission sorted through the delivery list. He was looking for something upbound. Mrs. Crowe would know what to do about Rodny. Maybe she could find out from the mayor what he was being punished for, perhaps put in a good word for him.

"Wait," he said, glancing up at Katelyn. "What do you mean he was in a good mood? And he was heading for *Supply?*" Mission thought of the job he'd been offered by Wyck. The head of IT had said Mission wouldn't be the last to hear of the offer. Maybe he hadn't been the *first*, either. "Where was Cam coming from?"

Katelyn touched her fingers to her tongue and flipped through the old log. "I think his last delivery was a broken computer heading to—"

"That little rat." Mission slapped the counter. "You got anything else heading down? Maybe to Supply or Chemical?"

She checked her computer, fingers clacking furiously, the rest of her perfectly serene. "We're so slow right now," she said apologetically. "I've got something from Mechanical back up to Supply. Forty five pounds. No rush. Standard freight." She peered across the counter at Mission, seeing if he was interested.

"I'll take it," he said. But he didn't plan on heading straight to Mechanical. If he raced, maybe he could beat Cam to Supply and do that other job for Wyck. That was the way in he was looking for. It wasn't the money he wanted, it was having an excuse to go back to thirty-four to collect his pay, another chance to see Rodny, see what kind of help his friend needed, what sort of trouble he was truly in.

·18·

Mission made record time downbound. It helped that traffic was light, but it wasn't a good sign that he didn't pass Cam on the way. The kid must've had a good head start. Either that, or Mission had gotten lucky and had overtaken the kid while he was off the stairway for a bathroom break.

Pausing for a moment on the landing outside of Supply, Mission caught his breath and dabbed the sweat from his neck. He still hadn't had his shower. Maybe after he found Cam and took care of this job in Mechanical, he could get cleaned up and get some proper rest. Lower Dispatch would have a change of clothes for him. And then he could figure out what to do about Rodny. So much to think about. A blessing that it took his mind off it being his birthday.

Inside Supply, he found a handful of people waiting at the counter. No sign of Cam. If the boy had come and gone already, he must've flown, and the delivery must've been heading further down. Mission tapped his foot and waited his turn. Once at the counter, he asked for Joyce, just like Wyck had said. The man helping him pointed to a heavyset woman with her hair up in a tight bun at the other end of the counter. Mission recognized her. She handled a lot of the flow of equipment marked special for IT. He waited until she was done with her customer, then asked for any deliveries under the name of Wyck.

She narrowed her eyes at him. "You got a glitch at Dispatch?" she asked. "Done handed that one off." She waved for the next person in line.

"Could you tell me where it was heading?" Mission asked. "I was sent to relieve the other guy. His . . . his mother is sick. They're not sure if she's gonna make it."

Mission winced at the lie. The lady behind the counter twisted her mouth in disbelief.

"Please," he begged. "It really is important."

She hesitated. "It was going six flights down to an apartment. I don't have the exact number. It was on the delivery report."

"Six down." Mission knew the level. Residential except for the handful of less-than-legal businesses being run out of a few apartments. "Thanks," he said. He slapped the counter and hurried toward the exit. It was on his way to Mechanical, anyway. He might be too late for Wyck's delivery, but he could ask Cam if he might pick up the pay for him, offer him a vacation chit in return. Or he could just flat out tell him an old friend was in trouble, and he needed to get through security. If not, he'd have to wait for an IT request to hit Dispatch and be the first to jump on it. And he'd have to hope that Rodny had that much time.

He was four levels down, formulating a dozen such plans, when the blast went off.

The great stairwell lurched as if thrown sideways. Mission slammed against the rail and nearly went over. He wrapped his arms around the trembling steel and held on.

There was a shriek, a chorus of groans. He watched, his head out in space beyond the railing, as the landing two levels below twisted away from the staircase. The metal sang and cried out as it was ripped free and went tumbling into the depths.

More than one body plummeted after. The receding figures performed cartwheels in space.

Mission tore himself away from the sight. A few steps down from him, a woman remained on her hands and knees, looking up at Mission with wild and frightened eyes. There was a distant crash, impossibly far below.

"I don't know," he wanted to say. There was that question in her eyes, the same one pounding in his skull, echoing with the sound of the blast. *What the hell just happened? Is this it? Has it begun?*

He considered running up, away from the calamity, but there were screams from below, and a porter had a duty to those on the stairwell in need. He helped the woman to her feet and bid her upward. Already, the smell of something acrid and the haze of smoke were upon them. "Go," he urged, and then he spiraled down against the sudden flow of traffic, responding on automatic to his shadowing days rather than to some deeply held sense of duty. And his friend. Cam was down there. Where the boy had gone and where the blast had occurred were still coincidence in Mission's rattled mind.

The landing below held a crush of people. Residents and shopkeeps crowded out of the doors and fought for a spot at the rail that they might gaze over at the wreckage one flight further down. Mission fought his way through, yelling Cam's name, keeping an eye out for his friend. A bedraggled couple staggered up to the crowded landing with hollow eyes, clutching the railing and each other. He didn't see Cam anywhere.

He raced down five turns of the central post, his normally deft feet stumbling on the slick treads, around and around. It'd been the level Cam was heading toward, right? Six down. Level one-sixteen. He would be okay. Mission convinced himself Cam would be okay. The sight of those people tumbling through the air flashed in Mission's mind. It was an image he knew he'd never forget. Surely, Cam wasn't among them. The boy was late or early to everything, never right on time.

He made the last turn, and where the next landing should've been was empty space. The stalwart rails of the great spiral staircase had been ripped outward before parting. A few of the steps sagged away from the central post, and gravity tugged at Mission's feet. He could feel a pull toward the edge, the void clawing at him. There was nothing there to stop him from going over. The steel felt slick beneath his boots.

Across a gap of torn and twisted steel, the doorway to one-sixteen was missing. In its place stood a pocket of crumbling cement and dark iron bars bent outward like hands reaching for the departed landing. White powder drifted down from the ceiling beyond the rubble. Unbelievably, there were sounds beyond the veil. Coughs and shouts. Screams for help.

People were yelling from the landing above as well. A fire hose slithered down, the nozzle clinking and banging against the wall of the stairwell. There was no one there to accept it, just an orange glow of fire deep inside that seemed to throb. It was as if the earth's chest had been torn open, exposing its bright red heartbeat, the bent rods of steel now like a shattered ribcage.

"Porter!" someone yelled from above.

Mission carefully slid to the edge of the sloping and bent steps. He held the railing where it had been torn free. It was warm to the touch. Leaning out, he studied the crowd fifty feet above him at the next landing. They were swinging the fire hose, trying to get it inside the busted door. But there was no landing rail to snag the nozzle on anymore, no one to grab it. Again, someone yelled something about a porter. Mission didn't know what was expected of him. He hadn't shadowed for this. The nozzle swung wildly a dozen feet away. Did they expect him to reach it? To swing over and douse that mad pulse in the heart of the burning earth?

Someone pointed when they spotted him leaning out, spotted the 'chief around his neck.

"There he is!" a woman shrieked, one of the mad-eyed women who had staggered past him as he hurried down, one of those who had survived. "The porter did it!" she yelled.

·19·

Mission froze, uncomprehending, even as the stairway thundered and clanged with a descending mob. The loosened treads beneath his feet shook. He reached for the inner post and clung to it for a moment. Across the smoke-hazed void, a figure appeared at the hole in the earth. Someone was alive inside level one-sixteen. A man with his undershirt pulled up over his mouth stared across at Mission with wide, horror-filled eyes.

Mission turned and ran. He stumbled downward, a hand on the inner post, watching for the return of the railing. So much had been pulled away. The stairs were unstable from the damage. He didn't know why he was running beyond that he was being chased. It took a full turn of the staircase for the railing to reappear and for him to feel safe at such speeds. It took just as long to realize that Cam was dead. His friend had delivered a package, and now he was dead. He and others. One glance at his blue 'chief, and someone above thought it'd been Mission who'd made the delivery. It very nearly had been.

Another crowd at landing one-seventeen. Tear-streaked faces, a woman trembling, her arms wrapped around herself, a man covering his face, all looking up or down beyond the rails. They had seen the wreckage tumble past. Mission hurried on. Lower Dispatch was all that lay between him and Mechanical that he might call haven. He hurried there, his mind still grasping for a handhold that'd been wrenched away. A violent scream approached from above and came much too fast.

Mission startled and nearly fell as the wailing person flew toward him. He waited for someone to tackle him from behind, but the sound whizzed past beyond the rail. Another person. Falling, alive and screaming, plummeting toward the depths. The loose steps and empty space had claimed one of those chasing him.

He quickened his pace, leaving the inner post for the outer rail where the curve of the steps was broader and smoother, where the force of his descent tugged him against the steel bar. Here, he could move faster. He tried not to think of what would happen if he came across a gap in the steel. He ran, smoke stinging his eyes, the clang and clamor of his own feet and that of distant others, not realizing at first that the haze in the air wasn't from the ruin he had left behind. The smoke all around him was *rising*.

• Silo 1 •

If you do not change direction,
you may end up where you are heading.

-Lao Tzu

·20·

onald's breakfast of powdered eggs and shredded potatoes had long grown cold. He rarely touched the food brought down by Thurman and Erskine, preferring instead the bland stuff in the unlabeled silver cans he had discovered among the storeroom's vacuum-sealed crates. It wasn't just the matter of trust—it was the rebelliousness of it all, the empowerment that came from foraging, from taking command of his own survival. He stabbed a yellowish-orange gelatinous blob that he assumed had once been part of a peach and put it in his mouth. He chewed, tasting nothing. He pretended it tasted like a peach.

Across the wide table, Anna fiddled with the dials on her radio and sipped loudly from a mug of cold coffee. A nest of wires ran from a black box to her computer, and a soft hiss of static filled the room. It was noise to Donald, but Anna squinted at a set of speakers and tilted her head like an animal with a higher sense. She seemed capable of listening to the indiscernible.

"It's too bad we can't get a better station," Donald said morosely. He speared another wedge of mystery fruit and popped it into his mouth. Mango, he told himself, just for variety.

"No station is the best station," she said, referring to her hope that the towers of Silo 40 and its neighbors would remain silent. She had tried to explain what she was doing to cut off unlikely survivors, but little of it made any sense to Donald. A year ago, supposedly, Silo 40 had hacked the system. It was assumed to have been a rogue Head of IT. No one else could be expected to possess the expertise and access required of such a feat. By the time the camera feeds were cut, every fail-safe had already been severed. Attempts to terminate the silo were made, but with no way to verify them. It was apparent these attempts had failed when the darkness began to spread to other silos.

Thurman, Erskine, and Victor had been woken according to protocol, one after the other. Further fail-safes proved ineffective, and Erskine worried the hacking had progressed to the level of the nanos, that everything was in jeopardy. After much cajoling, Thurman had convinced the other two that Anna could help. Her research at M.I.T. had been in wireless harmonics; remote charging technology; RFIDs; the ability to assume control of electronics via radio.

She'd eventually been able to commandeer the collapse mechanism of the afflicted silos. Donald still had nightmares thinking about it. While she described the process, he had studied the wall schematic of a standard silo. He had pictured the blasts that freed the layers of heavy concrete between the levels, sending them like dominoes down to the bottom, crushing everything and everyone in-between. Stacks of concrete fifty feet thick had been cut loose to turn entire societies into rubble. These underground buildings had been designed from the beginning so they could be brought down like any other—and remotely. The insight that such a fail-safe was even needed seemed as sick as the solution was cruel.

What now remained of those silos was all hiss and crackle, a chorus of ghosts. The silo Heads in the rest of the facilities hadn't even been told of the calamity. There would be no red Xs on their schematics to haunt their days. The various Heads had little contact with each other as it was. The greater worry was of panic spreading.

But everyone in Silo 1 knew. Victor had known. And Donald suspected it was this heavy burden that had led him to an unspeakable escape rather than any of the theories Thurman had offered. Thurman was so in awe of Victor's supposed brilliance that he searched for purpose behind his madness, some conspiratorial cause. Donald was verging on the sad realization that humanity had been thrown on the brink of extinction by insane men in positions of power following one another, each thinking the others knew where they were going.

He took a sip of tomato juice from a punctured can and reached for two pieces of paper amid the carpet of notes and reports surrounding his keyboard. The fate of a silo supposedly rested on something in these two pages. They were copies of the same report. One was a virgin printout of something he'd written long ago about the fall of another silo. Donald barely remembered writing it. And now he had stared at it so long, the meaning had been squeezed out of the ink. It had become like a word that, repeated, devolves into mere sound.

The other copy was of the notes Victor had scrawled across the face of this report. He had written his notes with a red pen, and someone upstairs had managed to pull just this color off in order to make both versions more legible. By copying the red, however, they had also transferred a fine mist and a few splatters. These marks were gruesome reminders that the report had been atop Victor's desk in the final moments of his life.

That could mean anything or nothing, Donald thought. In fact, after three days of study, he was beginning to suspect that the report was nothing more than a scrap of paper. Why else write across the top of it? And yet Victor had told Thurman several times that the key to quelling the violence in Silo 18 lay right there. He had argued strongly for Donald to be pulled from the deep freeze, but hadn't been able to get Erskine or Thurman to side with him. So this was all Donald had, a liar's account of what a dead man had said.

Liars and dead men—two parties unskilled at dispensing truth.

The scrap of paper with the red ink and rust-colored bloodstains offered little help. There were a few lines that resonated, however. They reminded Donald of how horoscopes were able to land vague and glancing blows, which gave credence to all their other feints.

"The One who remembers" had been written in bold and confident letters across the center of the report. Donald couldn't help but feel that this referred to him and his resistance to the medication. Hadn't Anna said that Victor spoke of him frequently, that he wanted him awake for testing or questioning? Other musings were vague and dire in equal measure. *"This is why,"* Victor had written. Also: *"An end to them all."*

Did he mean the why of his suicide or the why of Silo 18's violence? And an end to all of what?

In many ways, the cycle of violence in Silo 18 was no different than what took place elsewhere. Beyond being more severe, it was the same waxing and waning of the mobs, of each generation revolting against the last, a fifteen- to twenty-year cycle of bloody upheaval.

Victor had left reports behind about everything from primate behavior to the wars of the twentieth and twenty-first centuries.

There was one report that Donald found especially disturbing: it detailed how primates came of age and attempted to overthrow their fathers, the alpha males. It told of chimps that committed infanticide, males snatching the young from their mothers and taking them into the trees where their arms and legs were ripped, limb by limb, from their small bodies. Victor had written that this put the females back into estrus. It made room for the next generation.

Donald had a hard time believing any of this was true. He had a harder time making sense of a report about frontal lobes and how long they took to develop in humans. Maybe this was important to unraveling some mystery. Or perhaps it was the ravings of a man losing his mind, or a man discovering his conscience and coming to grips with what he'd done to the world. Or maybe it was because of Silo 40, from watching impotently while his grand and twisted plans crumbled into ruin.

Donald studied his old report and Victor's notes and saw the same bit of nothing. Anna thought a people could be saved by what the report contained. Thurman was impatient to terminate the silo now before the violence spilled to some neighbor. Donald was reminded of his story, of having killed a man to save others. He thought about how bombs were used to douse fires, nukes used to end wars, fires to fight fires. He wanted no part of such a decision.

And so he searched. He fell into a routine that Anna had long ago perfected. They slept, ate, and worked. They emptied bottles of scotch at night one burning sip at a time and left them standing like factory smokestacks amid the diagram of silos. In the mornings, they took turns with the lone shower that adjoined what seemed an executive's office. Or a general's office. Anna would be brazen with her nakedness, Donald wishing she wouldn't be. Her presence became an intoxicant from the past, and Donald began to confabulate a new reality in his mind: He and Anna were working on one more secret project together; Helen was back in Savannah; Mick wasn't making it to the meetings; Donald couldn't raise either of them because his cell phone wouldn't work.

It was always that his cell phone didn't work. Just one text getting through on the day of the convention, and Helen might be down in the deep freeze, asleep in her pod. He could visit her the way Erskine visited his daughter. They would be together again once all the shifts were over.

In another version of the same dream, Donald imagined that he was able to crest that hill and make it to the Tennessee side. Bombs exploded in the air, frightened people dove into their holes, a young girl sang with a voice so pure. In this fantasy, he and Helen disappeared into the same earth. They had children and grandchildren and were buried together.

Dreams such as these kept him sane as he slept and haunted him when he woke. They haunted him when he allowed Anna to touch him, to lay in his cot for an hour before bedtime, just the sound of her breathing, her head on his chest, the smell of alcohol on both their breaths, reminding him of college days. He would lay there and tolerate it, suffer how good it felt, her hand resting on his neck, and only fall asleep after she grew uncomfortable from the cramped quarters and moved back to her own cot.

In the morning, she would sing in the shower, steam billowing into the war room, while Donald returned to his studies. He would log onto her computer where he was able to dig through the files in Victor's personal directories. He could see when these files had been created, accessed, and how often. One of the oldest and most recently opened was a list with all the silos ranked. Number 18 was near the top, but it wasn't clear if this was a measure of trouble or worth. And why rank them to begin with? For what purpose?

He also used Anna's computer to search for his sister, Charlotte. She wasn't listed in the pods below, not under any name or picture that he could find. But she had been there during orientation. He remembered her being led off with so many others and being put to sleep. And now she seemed to have vanished. But where?

So many questions. He stared at the two reports, the awful sound of hissing ghosts leaking from the radio, and the weight of all the earth above him driving him mad. And he began to suspect that Silo 1 had certain fail-safes as well, that the lift took too long between levels, that a press of concrete hovered over all their heads that none of them could see. Such was his fear and his hope, two wildly different emotions that became difficult to distinguish as Donald followed Victor's messy trail. He began to wonder, if he followed this dead man too closely, if perhaps he would reach the same fateful conclusion in the end.

·21·

When he could no longer look at the notes and see anything but blood, Donald went for what had become his customary stroll among the guns and dozing drones. This was his escape from the hiss of Anna's work and the cramped confines of their makeshift home, and it was during these laps through the darkened storehouse that he came nearest to clearing his head from his dreams, from the prior night's bottle of scotch, and from the mix of emotions he was beginning to feel for Anna.

Most of all, he walked those laps and tried to make sense of this new world. He puzzled over what Thurman and Victor had planned for the silos. Five hundred years below ground, and then what? Donald desperately wanted to know. And here was when he felt truly alive: when he was taking action, when he was digging for answers. It was the same fleeting sense of power he had felt from refusing their pills, from staining his fingers purple and tonguing the ulcers that formed in his cheeks. It was the rattling of chains. Chains he could not hope to shake loose, but that he could shake nonetheless.

He passed the two lifts, feeling such courage, and tried both call buttons. He tried them several times a day, but neither would light without a badge. He was beginning to know the rules and secrets of that darkened place. In his explorations, he had discovered the plastic crate with the missing firearm, the one he assumed Victor had stolen. The airtight seal was broken, and the other guns inside reeked of grease. It seemed strange at first that he was a prisoner locked away with instruments of war, but then he realized that he and Anna had simply been cloistered away with all the other forbidden things. They had been tucked away where they wouldn't be discovered.

It hadn't kept him from prying open other crates to see what was inside. Some contained folded uniforms and suits like astronauts wore, all vacuum sealed in thick plastic. Another held helmets with large domes and metal collars. There were flashlights with red lenses, food and medical kits, backpacks, rounds and rounds of ammo, and myriad other devices and gadgets he could only guess at. The day before, he had found a laminated map in one crate, a chart of the fifty silos. There were red lines that radiated from the silos, one from each, and met at a single point in the distance. Donald had traced the lines with his finger, holding the map up to catch the light spilling from the distant offices. These things were puzzled over and put back in their place, clues to a mystery he couldn't define.

He stopped during his lap to perform a set of jumping jacks in the wide aisles between the sleeping drones. The exercise had been a struggle just two days ago, but the chill seemed to be melting from his veins. And the more he pushed himself, the more awake and alert he seemed to become. He did seventy-five, which was ten more than yesterday. After catching his breath, he dropped down to see how many pushups he could do on his atrophied muscles. And it was here, on the third day of his captivity, that he discovered the launch lift, a garage door that barely came to his waist but was wide enough for the wings that lurked beneath the tarps.

Donald rose from his pushup and approached the low door. The entire storehouse was kept incredibly dim, this wall almost pitch black. He thought about going for one of the flashlights when he saw the red handle. A tug, and the door slid up into the wall. On his hands and knees, Donald explored the cavity beyond, which went back over a dozen feet. There were no buttons or levers that he could feel along the walls, no method of operating the lift.

Curious, he crawled out and decided to grab a flashlight. Before he turned, however, he saw another door along the darkened wall, a door he'd never noticed before, one he assumed led to a closet or a mechanical space. Donald tried the handle and found it unlocked, a dim hallway beyond. He glanced toward the spill of light in the direction of the offices, a barely audible hiss emanating from Anna's work. Reaching inside the hall, he fumbled for a light switch, and the overhead bulbs flickered hesitantly. Shielding his eyes—having grown used to the darkness in the warehouse—he crept inside. He pulled the door shut behind him so as not to disturb the sleeping drones.

The hallway beyond possessed the eerie calm of a place haunted. It ran fifty paces to a door at the far end, with a pair of doors on either side. More offices, he assumed, similar to the small home Anna had carved out in the back of the warehouse. He tried the first door, and the odor of mothballs or some cleaning chemical wafted out. Inside, he discovered where his cot had come from.

There were rows of bunks, the shuffle of recent footsteps in a layer of dust, and a place where two small beds formerly lay. There were dressers built into the walls and a trunk at the foot of each bed. The absence of people could be felt. This was a place meant for the living, and Donald wondered briefly why the two cots had been removed at all, why not sleep here? His curiosity grew stronger as he peeked into the door across the hall and found bathroom stalls and a cluster of showers.

The next two doors were more of the same, except for a row of urinals in the bathroom. The sight of these made Donald need to go. He crept inside and tested one, was mildly surprised when it flushed and was startled by how loud it was. While he went, he had a fear that Anna was looking for him, that she might hear the water banging through the pipes and barge in.

He finished and flushed, then noted the layer of dust on the handle of the neighboring urinal. Perhaps this place had been taken off the maintenance rounds while Anna was awake. Maybe people had lived down here and kept up with the munitions once but had relocated to make room for her secret presence. But Donald didn't remember anyone coming to this level during his first shift. No, these were quarters kept for another time, much like the machines beneath the tarps. And rather than put Donald where it made the most sense, where there was plenty of room and a second shower, Anna had kept him in the suite she'd long ago made for herself. To keep him near, perhaps. And Donald wondered for the first time if he was awake not because he held the answer to any mystery, but simply because she wanted him to be.

He washed his hands and studied himself in the mirror. His eyes were red and puffy, his hair disheveled, his cheeks gaunt and bearing three days of growth. He was turning gray, he saw. The centuries spent asleep were aging him. He laughed at this, laughed at the idea that the man in the mirror was him at all, that he was still alive, his wife gone, that any of this were more than a dream. Flicking off the light, he left the bathroom to the ghosts and checked the door at the end of the hall.

Inside, he found furniture locked in ice, the light from the hallway shimmering as it caught what looked like massive cubes of frozen water. The illusion was dispelled as he fumbled for the switch. It was sheets of plastic thrown over tables and chairs, a fine mist of dust settled on top. Donald approached one of the tables and saw the computer display beneath the sheet. The chairs were attached to the desks, and there was something familiar about the knobs and levers. He knelt and fumbled for the edge of the plastic and peeled it up noisily. He turned and checked the empty hallway, unable to shake the feeling of others being present.

The flight controls he revealed took him back to another life. Here was the stick his sister had called a yoke, the pedals beneath the seat she had called something else, the throttle and all the other dials and indicators. Donald remembered touring her training facility after she graduated flight school. They had flown to Colorado for her ceremony. He remembered watching a screen just like this as her drone took to the air and joined a formation of others. He remembered the view of Colorado from the nose of her graceful machine in flight.

He glanced around the room at the dozen or so stations. The obvious need for the place slammed into what had felt like a secret discovery. He imagined voices in the hallway, men and women showering and chatting, towels being snapped at asses, someone looking to borrow a razor, a shift of pilots sitting at these desks where coffee could lie perfectly still in steaming mugs as death was rained down from above.

Donald returned the plastic sheet. Dust shivered off and ran down the gleaming material like an avalanche on a snowy hillside. He thought of his sister, asleep and hidden some levels below where he couldn't find her, and he wondered if she hadn't been brought there as a surprise for him at all. Maybe she had been brought as a surprise for some future *others*.

And suddenly, thinking of her, thinking of a time lost to dreams and lonely tears, Donald found himself patting his pockets in search of something. Pills. An old prescription with her name on it. Helen had forced him to see a doctor, hadn't she? And Donald suddenly knew why he couldn't forget, why their drugs didn't work on him. The realization came with a powerful longing to see his sister. Charlotte was the why. She was the answer to one of Thurman's riddles.

·22·

"I want to see her first," Donald demanded. "Let me see her, and then I'll tell you."

He waited for Thurman or Dr. Henson to reply. The three of them stood in Henson's office on the cryopod wing. Donald had bargained his way down the lift with Thurman, and now he bargained further. His sister was the answer to why he couldn't forget. He would exchange that answer for another. He wanted to know where she was, to see her.

Something unspoken passed between the two men. Thurman turned to Donald with a warning. "She will not be woken," he said. "Not even for this."

Donald nodded. He saw how only those who made the laws were allowed to break them.

Henson turned to the computer on his desk. "I'll look her up."

"No need," Thurman said. "I know where she is."

He led them out of the office and down the hall, past the main shift rooms where Donald had awoken as Troy all those years ago, past the deep freeze where he had spent nearly a century asleep, all the way to another door just like the others.

The code Thurman entered was different; Donald could tell by the discordant four-note song the buttons made. Above the keypad in small stenciled letters he made out the words: *Emergency Personnel.* Locks whirred and ground like old bones, and the door gradually opened.

Steam followed them inside, the warm air from the hallway hitting the mortuary cool. There were fewer than a dozen rows of pods, perhaps fifty or sixty units total, little more than a full shift. Donald peered into one of the coffin-like units, the ice a spiderweb of blue and white on the glass, and saw inside a thick and chiseled visage. A frozen soldier, or so his imagination informed him.

Thurman led them through the rows and columns before stopping at one of the pods. He rested his hands on its surface with something like affection. His exhalations billowed into the air. It made his white hair and stark beard appear as though they were frosted with ice.

"Charlotte," Donald breathed, peering in at his sister. She hadn't changed, hadn't aged a bit. Even the blue cast of her skin seemed normal and expected, as he was growing used to seeing people this way.

He rubbed the small window to clear the web of frost and marveled at his thin hands and seemingly fragile joints. He had atrophied. He had grown older while his sister remained the same.

"I locked her away like this once," he said, gazing in at her. "I locked her away in my memory like this when she went off to war. Our parents did the same. She was just little Charla. She was over there flying planes with her joystick like the video games she used to play."

He thought of Charlotte in front of her computer as a kid. He had thought she was overseas doing something innocent like that.

Glancing away from her, he studied the two men on the other side of the pod. Henson started to say something, but Thurman placed a hand on the doctor's arm. Donald turned back to his sister.

"Of course, it wasn't a game. She was killing people. We talked about it years later, after I was in office and she'd figured I'd grown up enough." He laughed and shook his head. "My kid sister, waiting for *me* to grow up."

A tear plummeted to the frozen pane of glass. The salt cut through the ice and left a clear track behind. Donald wiped it away with a squeak, then felt frightened he might disturb her.

"They would get her up in the middle of the night," he said. "Whenever a target was deemed . . . what did she call it? *Actionable*. They would get her up. She said it was strange to go from dreaming to killing, how none of it made sense, how she would go back to sleep and see the video feeds in her mind—that last view from a missile's nose as she guided it into its target—"

He took a breath and gazed up at Thurman.

"I thought it was good that she couldn't be hurt, you know? She was safe in a trailer somewhere, not up there in the sky. But she complained about it. She told her doctor that it didn't feel right, being safe and doing what she did. The people on the front lines, they had fear as an excuse. They had self-preservation. A reason to kill. Charlotte used to kill people and then go to the mess hall and eat a piece of pie. That's what she told her doctor. She would eat something sweet and not be able to taste it."

"What doctor was this?" Henson asked.

"My doctor," Donald said. He wiped his cheek, but he wasn't ashamed of the tears. Being by his sister's side had him feeling brave and bold, less alone. He could face the past and the future, both.

"Helen was worried about my reelection," he explained. "Charlotte already had a prescription, had been diagnosed with PTSD after her first tour, and so we kept filling it under her name, even under her insurance."

Henson waved his hand, stirring the air for more information. "What prescription?"

"Propra," Thurman said. "She'd been taking Propra, hadn't she? And you were worried about the press finding out."

Donald nodded. "Helen was worried. She thought it might come out that I was taking medication for my . . . wilder thoughts. The pills helped me forget them, kept me level. I could study the Order, and all I saw were the words, not the implications. There was no fear." He looked at his sister, understanding finally why she had refused to take the meds. She *wanted* the fear. It was necessary somehow. The medication they'd prescribed was the exact opposite of what she needed.

"I remember you telling me she was on them." Thurman said. "We were in the bookstore—"

"Do you remember your dosage?" Henson asked. "How long were you on it?"

"I started taking it after I was given the Order to read." He watched Thurman for any hint of expression and got nothing. "I guess that was two or three years before the convention. I took them nearly every day right up until then." He turned to Henson. "I would've had some on me during orientation if I hadn't lost them on the hill that day. I think I fell. I remember falling—"

Henson turned to Thurman. "There's no telling what the complications might be. Victor was careful to screen psychotropics from administrative personnel. Everyone was tested—"

"I wasn't," Donald said.

Henson faced him. "Everyone was tested."

"Not him." Thurman studied the surface of the pod, spoke to Henson. "There was a last minute change. A switch. I vouched for him. And if he was taking her meds, there wouldn't have been anything in his medical records."

"We need to tell Erskine," Henson said. "I could work with him. We might come up with a new formulation." He turned away from the pod like he needed to get back to his office.

Thurman looked to Donald. "Do you need more time down here?"

Donald studied his sister a moment. He wanted to wake her, to talk to her. Maybe he could come back another time just to visit.

"I might like to come back," he said.

"We'll see."

Thurman walked around the pod and placed a hand on Donald's shoulder, gave him a light, sympathetic squeeze. He led Donald away from the pod and toward the door, and Donald didn't glance back, didn't check the screen for his sister's new name. He didn't care. He knew where she was, and she would always be Charlotte to him. She would never change.

"You did good," Thurman said. "This is real good." They stepped into the hall and closed the thick doors with their massive locks. "You may have stumbled on why Victor was so obsessed with that report of yours."

"I did?" Donald didn't see the connection.

"I don't think he was interested in what you wrote at all," Thurman said. "I think he was interested in *you*."

·23·

They rode the lift toward the cafeteria rather than drop Donald off on fifty-five. It was almost dinnertime, and he could help Thurman with the trays. While the lights behind the level numbers blinked on and off, following their progress up the shaft, the idea that Thurman might be right haunted him. What if Victor had been curious about his resistance to the medication? What if it wasn't anything in that report at all?

They rode past level 40, its button winking bright and then going dark, and Donald thought of the silo that had done the same. "What does this mean for 18?" he asked, watching the next number flash by.

Thurman stared at the stainless steel doors, a greasy palm print there from where someone had caught their balance.

"Vic wanted to try another reset on 18," he said. "I never saw the point. But after his death—" Thurman hesitated. "Maybe we give them one more chance."

"What's involved in a reset?"

"You know what's involved." Thurman faced him. "It's what we did to the world, just on a smaller scale. Reduce the population, wipe the computers, their memories, try it all over again. We've done that several times before with this silo. There are risks involved. You can't create trauma without making a mess. At some point, it's simpler and safer to pull the plug."

"End them," Donald said, and he saw what Victor had been up against, what he had worked to avert. He wished he could speak to the old man, now that he knew what he knew. Anna said Victor had spoken of him often. And Erskine had said he wished people like Donald were in charge. What did that mean, all that nonsense about names being all that mattered and doing what was right for a change?

The elevator opened on the top level. Donald stepped out, and it was strange to walk among those on their shift, to be present and at the same time invisible, a body moving among the chatter while not a part of it all.

He noticed that no one here looked to Thurman with deference. He was not that shift's head, and no one knew him as such. They were just two men, one in white and one in beige, grabbing food and glancing at the ruined wasteland on the wallscreen.

Donald took one of the trays and noticed again that most people sat facing the view. Only one or two ate with their backs to it, preferring not to see. He followed Thurman back to the elevator while longing to speak to these handful, to ask them what they remembered, what they were afraid of, to tell them that it was okay to be afraid.

"Why do the other silos have screens?" he asked Thurman, keeping his voice down. The parts of the facility he'd had no hand in designing made little sense to him. "Why show them what we did?"

"To keep them in," Thurman said. He balanced the tray with one hand and pressed the call button on the express. "It's not that we're showing them what we did. We're showing them what's out there. Those screens and a few taboos are all that contain these people. Humans have this disease, Donny, this compulsion to move until we bump into something. And then we tunnel through that something, or we sail over the edge of the oceans, or we stagger across mountains—"

The elevator arrived. A man in reactor red excused himself and stepped between the two. They boarded, and Thurman fumbled for his badge. "Fear," he said. "Even the fear of death is barely enough to counter this compulsion of ours. If we didn't show them what was there, they would go look for themselves. That's what we've always done."

Donald considered this. He thought about his own desire, his mad urge, to escape the confines of all that pressing concrete. Even if it meant death out there. The slow strangulation was worse, he decided. It was all about choosing the lesser of two evils.

"I'd rather see a reset than extinguish the entire silo," he said, watching the numbers race by. He didn't mention that he'd been reading up on the people who lived there. Bad things would happen to many of them, but there would be a chance at life afterward.

"I'm less and less eager to gas the place, myself," Thurman admitted. "When Vic was around, all I did was argue against wasting our time with any one silo like this. Now that he's gone, I find myself pulling for these people. It's like I have to honor his last wishes. And that's a dangerous trap to fall into."

The elevator stopped on twenty and picked up two workers, who ceased a conversation of their own and fell silent for the ride. Donald thought about this process of cleansing a silo only to watch the violence repeat itself. The great wars he remembered from the old days came like this, a new generation unremembering, so that sons marched into the wars their fathers had fought before them.

The two workers got off at the rec hall, resuming their conversation as the doors closed. Donald remembered how much he enjoyed punishing himself in the weight room. Now he was wasting away with little appetite, nothing to push against, no resistance.

"It makes me wonder sometimes if that was why he did what he did," Thurman said. The elevator slid toward fifty-five. "Vic calculated everything. Always with a purpose. Maybe his way of winning this argument of ours was to ensure he had the last word." Thurman glanced at Donald. "Hell, it's what finally got me to agree to wake you up."

Donald didn't say out loud how crazy that sounded. He thought Thurman just needed some way to make sense of the unthinkable. Of course, there was another way Victor's death had ended the argument. Not for the first time, Donald imagined that it hadn't been a suicide at all. But he didn't see where such doubts could get him except in trouble.

They got off on fifty-five and carried the trays through the aisles of munitions. As they passed the sleeping drones, Donald thought of his sister, similarly sleeping. It was good to know where she was, that she was safe. A small comfort.

They ate at the war table. Donald pushed his dinner around his plate while Thurman and Anna talked. The two reports sat before him, constant companions, a bevy of notes with a splatter of blood, a report that he'd been reading too much into, notes about him remembering, about this being the great *why* of it all.

Just a scrap of paper, he thought. No mystery. He had been looking at the wrong thing, assuming there was a clue in the words, but it was just Donald's *existence* that Victor had remarked upon. He had sat across the hall from Donald and watched him react to whatever was in their water or their pills. Victor had watched him go mad. And now when Donald looked at his notes, all he saw was a piece of paper with pain scrawled across it amid specks of blood. Blood that had been copied over with the handwritten notes, both now black as copier toner.

Ignore the blood, he told himself. The blood wasn't a clue. It had come after. There were several splatters in a wide space left in the notes. Donald had been studying the senseless. He had been looking for something that wasn't there. He may as well have been staring off into space.

Space. Donald set his fork down and grabbed the other report. Once you ignored the large spots of blood, there was a hole, a vacancy where nothing had been written. This was what he should've been focused on. Not what was there, but what wasn't.

He checked the other report—the corresponding location of that blank space—to see what was written there. He was grasping at air, he knew. Sure enough, when he found the right spot, his excitement vanished. It was the paragraph that didn't belong, the one about the young inductee whose great grandmother remembered the old times. It was nothing.

Unless—

Donald sat up straight. Thurman had said the report wasn't about its contents at all. But maybe they had been looking at the *wrong contents*. He took the two reports and placed them on top of each other. Anna was telling Thurman about her progress with the jamming of the radio towers, that she would be done soon. Thurman was saying that they could all get off shift in the next few days, get the schedule back in order. Donald held the overlapping reports up to the lights. Thurman looked on curiously.

"He wrote *around* something," Donald muttered. "Not *over* something."

He met Thurman's gaze and smiled. "You were wrong." The two pieces of paper trembled in his hands. "There is something here. He wasn't interested in me at all."

Anna set down her utensils and leaned over to have a look.

"If I had the original, I would've seen it straight away." He pointed to the space in the notes, then slid the top page away and tapped his finger on the one paragraph that didn't belong. The one that had nothing to do with Silo 12 at all.

"Here's why your resets don't work," he said. Anna grabbed the bottom report and read about the shadow Donald had inducted, the one whose great-grandmother remembered the old days, the one who had asked him a question about whether those stories were true.

"Someone in Silo 18 remembers," Donald said with confidence. "Maybe a bunch of people do, passing the knowledge down in secret from generation to generation. Or they're immune like me. They remember."

Thurman took a sip of his water. He set down the glass and glanced from his daughter to Donald. "More reason to pull the plug," he said.

"No," Donald told him. "No. That's not what Victor thought." He tapped the dead man's notes. "He wanted to find the one who remembers, but he didn't mean me." He turned to Anna. "I don't think he wanted me up at all. This isn't about me."

Anna looked up at her father, a puzzled expression on her face. She turned to Donald. "Are you saying there's another way?"

"Yes." He stood and paced behind the chairs, stepping over the wires that snaked across the tiles. "We need to call 18 and ask the head there if anyone fits this profile, someone or some group sowing discord, maybe talking about the world we—" He stopped himself from saying *destroyed*.

"Okay," Anna said, nodding her head. "Okay. Let's say they do know. Let's say we find these people over there like you. What then?"

He stopped his pacing. This was the part he hadn't considered. He found Thurman studying him, the old man's lips pursed.

"We find these people—" Donald said.

And he knew. He knew Thurman had been right. There was that story of a medic wounded, there was Donald's frustration with what had been done to the world. He imagined what it might take to save these people in this distant silo, these welders and shopkeeps and metalsmiths and their young shadows. He remembered being the one on a previous shift to press that button, to kill in order to save.

And he knew he would do it again.

• Silo 18 •

Hush, my child, too late to cry
The skies are dark, the rivers dry
Our parents gave us lives to keep
Buried here beneath the deep

They sent us down below the dirt
They lied and said it wouldn't hurt
Their lies still shield us from our dread
Buried here beside our dead

We cannot leave, we must not cry
We'll show them that our cheeks are dry
Now sleep, my child, accept the dream
Buried here, unless you clean

-Mary Fonvielle, age 22

·24·

Mission's throat itched and his eyes stung, the smoke growing heavier and the stench stronger as he approached Lower Dispatch. At least the pursuit from above seemed to have faltered, perhaps from the gap in the rails that had claimed a life.

Cam was gone, of that he felt certain. How many others? A twinge of guilt accompanied the sick thought that the fallen would have to be carried up to the farms in plastic bags. Someone would have to do that job, and it wouldn't be a pretty one.

He shook this thought away as he got within a level of Dispatch. Tears streamed down his face and mixed with the sweat and grime of the long day's descent. He bore bad news. A shower and clean clothes would do little to alleviate the weariness he felt, but there would be protection here, help in clearing up the confusion about the blast. He hurried down the last half flight and remembered, perhaps due to the rising ash that reminded him of a note he'd torn to confetti, the reason he'd been chasing after Cam in the first place.

Rodny. His friend was locked away in IT, and his plea for help had been lost in the din and confusion of the explosion.

The explosion. Cam. The package. The *delivery*.

Mission wobbled and clutched the railing for balance. He thought of the ridiculous fee for the delivery, a fee that perhaps was never meant to be paid. He gathered himself and hurried on, wondering what in the depths was going on, what kind of trouble his friend might be in, and how to help him. How, even, to *get* to him.

The air grew thick and it burned to breathe as he arrived at Dispatch. A small crowd huddled on the stairway. They peered across the landing and into the open doors of one-twenty-two. Mission coughed into his fist as he pushed his way through the gawkers. Had the wreckage from above landed here? Everything seemed intact. Two buckets lay on their sides near the door, and a gray fire hose snaked over the railing and trailed inside. A blanket of smoke clung to the ceiling; it trailed out and up the wall of the stairwell shaft like water from a giant faucet defying gravity.

Mission pulled his 'chief up over his nose, confused. The smoke was coming from *inside*. He breathed in through his mouth, the fabric pressing against his lips and lessening the sting in his throat. Dark shapes moved inside the hallway. He unsnapped the strap that held his knife in place and crossed the threshold, keeping low to stay away from the smoke.

Eli, one of the senior dispatchers, met him in the hall. He had a basket of scorched paper in his hands, a mournful look on his face. The floors were everywhere wet and squished with the traffic from deeper inside. It was dark, but cones of light danced around like fretful things.

"Look what you've done," Eli cried to Mission. "Look what you've done."

Mission hurried past him and toward the flashlights. The smoke was thicker, the water on the floor deeper. Bits of pulp worth saving floated on the surface. He passed one of the dormitories, the sorting hall, the front offices.

Lily, an elder porter, ran by in slaps and spray, recognizable only at the last moment as the beam from her flashlight briefly lit her face. There was someone lying in the water, pressed up against the wall. As Mission approached and a passing light played over the form, he saw that they weren't lying there at all. It was Hackett, one of the few dispatchers who treated the young shadows with respect and never seemed to take delight in their burdens. The glimpse Mission got revealed half a face recognizable, the other half à red blister. Deathdays. Lottery numbers flashed in Mission's vision.

"Porter! Get over here."

It was Morgan's voice. The old man's cough joined a chorus of others. The hallway was full of ripples and waves, splashes and hacks, smoke and commands. Mission hurried toward the familiar silhouette, his eyes burning.

"Sir? It's Mission. The explosion—" He pointed toward the ceiling.

"I know my own shadows, boy." A light was trained on Mission's eyes, a physical lash of sorts. "Get in here and give these lads a hand."

The smell of cooked beans and burnt and wet paper was overpowering. There was a hint of fuel behind it all, a smell Mission knew from the Down Deep and its generators. He had lugged a massive filter once that reeked of this. And there was something else: the smell of the bazaar during a pig roast, a foul and unpleasant odor.

The water in the main hall was deep. It lapped up over Mission's halfboots and filled them with muck. Drawers of files were being emptied into buckets. An empty crate was shoved into his hands, cones of light swirling in the mist, shapes moving and kicking up splashes, his nose burning and running, tears on his cheeks unbidden.

"Here, here," someone said, urging him forward. They warned him not to touch the filing cabinet. Piles of paper went into the crate, heavier than they should be. Mission didn't understand the rush. The fire was out. The walls were black where the flames must've licked them with their orange tongues, and the grow plots along the far wall where rows of beans had run up tall trestles were all ash. The trestles stood like black fingers, those that stood at all.

The porter beside him, Mission couldn't see who, cursed the farmers before leaving with a load. Amanda was there at the filing cabinet, her 'chief wrapped around her hand, managing the drawers as they were emptied. The crate filled up fast. Mission spotted someone emptying the wall safe of its old books as he turned back toward the hallway. There was a body in the corner covered in a sheet. Nobody was in as much of a hurry to remove that.

He followed the others toward the landing, but they did not go all the way out. The emergency lights in the dorm room were on, mattresses stacked up in the corner. Carter, Lyn, and Jocelyn were spreading the files out on the springs. Mission unloaded his crate and went back for another load. He asked Amanda what had happened, if this was retribution of some sort.

"They came for the beans," she said. She used her 'chief to wrestle with another drawer. "They came for the beans, and they burned it all."

Mission took in the wide swath of damage. He recalled how the stairwell had trembled during the blast, still saw the bodies falling and screaming to their deaths. Something was going on. The months of small violences had ramped up like a switch had been flipped. He wasn't convinced that this was about the beans at all.

• • • •

"So what do we do now?" Carter asked. He was a powerful porter, in his early thirties where men find their strength and have yet to lose their joints, but he looked absolutely beat. His hair clung to his forehead in wet clumps. There were black smears on his face, and you could no longer tell what color his 'chief had been. All signs that he had been present for and had fought back the fire.

"Now we burn their crops," someone suggested.

"The crops we eat?"

"Just the upper farms. They're the ones that did this."

"We don't know who did this," Morgan said.

Mission caught his old caster's eye. "In the storehouse," he said. "I saw— Was that—?"

Morgan nodded. "Hendricks. Aye."

Carter slapped the wall and barked profanities. "I'll kill 'em!" he yelled.

"So you're . . ." Mission wanted to say *Lower Chief*, but it was too soon for that to make sense.

"Aye," Morgan said, and Mission could tell it made little sense to him as well.

"People will be carrying whatever they like for a few days," Joel said. He coughed into his palm while Lyn looked on with concern. "We'll appear weak if we don't strike back."

Mission had other concerns besides appearing weak. The people above thought a porter had attacked them. And now this with the farmers, so far from where they'd been hit the night before. Porters were the nearest thing to a roaming sentry, and they were being knocked out by someone, purposefully he thought. There were all those boys being recruited into IT. It wasn't computers they were being hired to fix. It was something else.

"I need to get home," Mission said. It was a slip. He meant to say Up Top. He worked to unknot his 'chief. The thing reeked of smoke, as did his hands and his coveralls. He would need to find another color to don. He needed to get in touch with his friends.

"What do you think you're doing?" Morgan asked. His former caster seemed ready to say something else as Mission tugged the 'chief away. Instead, the old man's eyes fell to the bright red whelp around Mission's neck, the stain of a rope's embrace.

"I don't think this is about us at all," he said. "I think this is bigger than that. A friend of mine's in trouble. He's at the heart of all that's going wrong. I think something bad is going to happen to him or that he might know something. They won't let him talk to anyone."

"Rodny?" Lyn asked. She and Joel had been two years ahead of him, but they both knew he and Rodny from the Nest.

He nodded. "And Cam is dead," he told the others. He explained what'd happened on his way down, the blast, the people chasing him, the gap in the rails. Hands covered gaping mouths. Someone whispered Cam's name in disbelief. "I don't think anyone cares that we know," Mission added. "I think that's the point. Everyone's supposed to be angry. As angry as possible."

"I need time to think," Morgan said. "To plan."

"I don't know that there is much time," Mission said. He told them about the new hires at IT. He told Morgan about seeing Bradley there, about the young porter applying for a different job.

"What do we do?" Lyn asked, looking to Joel and the others.

"We take it easy," Morgan said, but he didn't seem so sure. The confidence he displayed as a senior porter and caster seemed shaken now that he was a chief. It was how knees got wobbly when that last bit of weight went onto a heavy load.

"I can't stay down here," Mission said flatly. "You can have every vacation chit I own, but I've got to get up-top. I don't know how, but I have to."

·25·

Before he went anywhere, Mission needed to get in touch with friends he could trust, anyone who might be able to help, the old gang from the Nest. As Morgan urged everyone on the landing back to work, Mission slunk down the dark and smoky hallway toward the sorting room, which had a computer he might use. Lyn and Joel followed, more eager to help Rodny than to clean up after the fire.

They checked the monitor at the sorting counter and saw that the computer was down, possibly from the power outage the night before. Mission remembered all those people with their broken computers earlier that morning at IT and wondered if there would be a working machine anywhere on five levels. Since he couldn't send a wire, he picked up the hard line to the other Dispatch offices to see if they could get a message out for him.

He tried Central, first. Lyn stood with him at the counter, her flashlight illuminating the dials and highlighting the haze of smoke in the room. Joel splashed among the shelves, moving the reusable sorting crates on the bottom higher up to keep them from getting wet. There was no response from Central.

"Maybe the fire got the radio, too," she whispered.

Mission didn't think so. The power light was on and the thing was making that crackling sound when he squeezed the button. He heard Morgan splash past in the hallway, yelling and complaining that his workforce was disappearing. Lyn cupped her hand over her flashlight. "Something is going on at Central," he told Lyn. He had a bad feeling.

The second waystation he tried up-top finally won a response. "Who's this?" someone asked with none of the formality nor the jargon radio operators were known for.

"This is Mission. Who's this?"

"Mission? You're in big trouble, man."

Mission glanced at Lyn. "Who is this?" he asked.

"This is Robbie. They left me alone up here, man. I haven't heard from anybody. But everyone's looking for you. What's going on down there?"

Joel stopped with the crates and trained his flashlight on the counter.

"Everyone's looking for me?" Mission asked.

"You and Cam, a few of the others. There was some kind of fight at Central. Were you there for that? I can't get word from anyone!"

Mission told him to calm down, which seemed an unfair thing to expect when he could hardly think straight himself. "Robbie, I need you to get in touch with some friends of mine. Can you send out wires? Something's wrong with our computers down here."

"No, ours are all kind of sideways. We've been having to use the terminal up at the mayor's office."

"The mayor's office? Okay, I need you to send a couple of wires, then. You got something to write with?"

"Wait," Robbie said. "These are official wires, right? If not, I don't have the authority—"

"Damnit, Robbie, this is important! Grab something to write with. I'll pay you back. They can dock me for it if they want." Mission glanced up at Lyn, who was shaking her head in disbelief. He coughed into his fist, the smoke tickling his throat. They should be *moving*, not explaining this to someone else.

"All right, all right," Robbie said. "Who'm I sending this to? And you owe me for this piece of paper because it's all I have to write on."

Mission let go of the transmit button to curse the kid. Joel laughed from behind the sorting stacks. Composing himself a moment, Mission thought about who would be most likely to get a wire and send it along to the others. He ended up giving Robbie three names, then told him what to write. He would have his friends meet him at the Nest, or meet each other if he couldn't make it there himself. The Nest had to be safe. Nobody would mess with the school or the Crow. Once the gang was together, they could figure out what to do. Maybe the Crow would know what to do. The hardest part for Mission would be figuring out how to join them.

"You got all that?" he asked Robbie, when the boy didn't reply.

"Yeah, yeah, man. I think you're gonna be over the character limit, though. This better come out of your pay."

"You've gotta be kidding me," Mission said, careful to release the mic first.

"Now what?" Lyn asked as he hung up the receiver. She played her flashlight around the sorting room, the beam catching in the smoke and dancing across the ripples in the water. Joel's boots had thrown the wet film into chaos. He had gotten most of the sorting crates moved up so they wouldn't get wet.

"I need coveralls," Mission said. He splashed around the counter and joined Joel by the shelves, began looking through the nearest crates. "They're looking for me, so I'm gonna need new colors if I'm getting up there."

"We," Lyn told him. "We need new colors. If you're going to the Nest, I'm coming with you."

"Me too," Joel said.

"I appreciate that," Mission said, "but company might make it more dangerous. We'd be more conspicuous."

"Yeah, but they're looking for you," Lyn said.

"Hey, we have a ton of these new whites." Joel pulled the lid off a sorting bin. "But they'll just make us stand out, won't they?"

"Whites?" Mission headed over to see what Joel was talking about.

"Yeah. For Security. We've been moving a ton of these lately. Came down from Garment a few days ago. No idea why they made up so many."

Mission checked the coveralls. The ones on top were covered in soot, more gray than white. There were dozens of them stacked in the reusable sorting crate. He remembered all the new hires. It was like they wanted half the silo to be dressed in white, the other half fighting one another. It made no sense. Unless the goal was simply to get everyone dead.

"Dead," Mission said out loud.

The others swung their flashlights at him. Mission was already splashing down the shelves to another crate. "I've got a better idea," he called out. A coughing fit seized him as he found the right bin. He and Cam had been given one of these just a few days ago. He reached in and pulled out a bag. "How would you two like to make some money?"

Joel and Lyn hurried over to see what he'd found, and Mission held up one of the heavy plastic bags with the bright silver zipper and the hauling straps.

"Three-hundred and eighty-four chits to divide between you," he promised. "Every chit I own. I just need you for one last tandem."

The two porters played their lights across the object in his hands. It was a black bag. A black bag made for hauls such as these.

·26·

The ground was too wet to roll it out proper, so Mission used the main counter, instead. He promised Lyn and Joel that he would transfer every chit in his account as soon as they got to a working computer. Joel told him to save his breath. They were just as eager as he was to get to higher levels. The bag, with all of death's taboo, would afford protection to them all.

Lyn worked the bright zipper loose, and Joel peeled the flaps back. Mission sat on the counter and worked the laces on his boots free. They were soaked, his socks as well. He shucked them off to keep the water out of the bag and to save the weight. Always a porter, thinking about weight. Lyn handed him one of the Security coveralls, an extra precaution. He wiggled out of his porter blues and tugged the whites on while Lyn looked the other way. His knife, he strapped back to his waist.

Outside, flashlights danced in the main hall, the other porters still recovering from the damage wrought by fire and flood. Mission coughed into his palm and snapped up the coveralls, which were at least a size too big for him. "You guys sure you're up for this?" he asked.

Lyn helped him slide his feet into the bag and worked the inside straps around his ankles. Never before had a corpse made it so easy. "Are *you* sure?" she asked, cinching the straps tight.

Mission laughed, his stomach fluttering with nerves. He stretched out and let them work the top straps under his shoulders. It felt surreal to be placing himself inside one of the bags. He had never heard of anyone getting in one willingly.

"Have you both eaten?" he asked.

"We'll be fine," Joel said. "Stop worrying."

"If it gets late—"

"Lie your head back," Lyn told him. She began working the zipper from his feet. "And don't talk unless we tell you it's okay. You'll have people jumping the rails out there if they hear you or see you move."

"We'll take a break every twenty or so," Joel added. "We'll bring you into a restroom with us. You can stretch and get some water."

Mission lifted a hand out to stop the zipper from passing his stomach. "Don't mention water," he said. He listened to the sounds of lapping ripples against the counter, the squish of the other two porters moving about in their boots. He begged his bladder to ignore the cues.

"Get your hand inside," Lyn told him. She worked the zipper up over his chest to his chin, hesitated, then kissed the pads of her fingers and touched his forehead the same way he'd seen countless loved ones and priests bless the dead. "May your steps rise to the heavens," she whispered.

Her wan smile caught in the spill of Joel's flashlight before the bag was sealed up over Mission's face.

"Or at least until Upper Dispatch," Joel added.

••••

Getting out of the lower waystation proved simple. Their fellow porters made way for the dead, maybe thinking Roker was the one in the bag. Several hands reached out and touched Mission through the plastic, showing respect, and he fought not to flinch nor cough. It felt as though the smoke was trapped in the bag with him. It pervaded his hair and skin, despite the brand new coveralls.

Joel took the lead, which meant Mission's shoulders were pressed against his. He faced upward, his body swaying in time to their steps, the straps beneath his armpits pulling the opposite way he was used to. It grew more comfortable as they hit the stairs and began the long spiral up. His feet were lowered until the blood no longer pooled in his head. Lyn carried her half of his weight from several steps below.

The dark and quiet overtook him as they left the chaos of the waystation. The two porters didn't talk as some tandems might. They saved their lungs and kept their thoughts to themselves. Joel set an aggressive pace. Mission could almost hear Morgan's metronome ticking, that silver arm that rocked back and forth with the time. Mission was that arm, now. He could sense the pace in his own gentle swaying, his body suspended in space above the steel treads.

As the steps passed, the intolerableness grew. It wasn't the difficulty breathing, for he had been shadowed well to manage his lungs on a long climb. And he could handle the stuffiness with the plastic pressed against his face. Nor was it the dark; his favorite hour for porting had always been the dim-time, being alone with his thoughts, stirring while others slept. It wasn't the stench of plastic and smoke, the tickle in his throat, or the pain of the straps.

It took several spirals around the central post to put his finger on what discomforted him so, what caused a hollow pit to form in his stomach, a likewise gaping void in his chest, that mix of feelings he got when he had free time and nothing to fill it with. His entire body felt like his legs sometimes did when they needed to twitch but he forced them still. It was an anxiety, and one that went beyond fearing for his friends, beyond the death of Cam, beyond the terror of a silo crumbling down around him. He placed the sensation as he listened to Joel's heavy and steady breathing, as he felt in his motionless legs the work and agony of his friends', as he endured doing nothing while they hauled his burdens. This was what Mission felt knotting his gut above all else: It was the act of lying still. Of being carried.

He was a burden. A burden.

The straps pinched his shoulders until his arms fell numb, and he swayed in the darkness, the sounds of boots on steel, of breathing, as he was lifted toward the heavens. Too great a burden. This was his weakness, his inability to be carried.

Mission felt like sobbing—but the tears would not come. He thought of his mother carrying him for all those months, no one to tell and no one to support her. Not until his father found out, and by then it was too late. He wondered how long his father had hated the bulge in her belly, how long he had wanted to cut Mission out like some cancer. Until it was too late and this was all his dad was left with, a tumor to raise, a reminder. Mission had never asked to be carried like that. And he had never wanted to be ported by anyone ever again.

Two years ago to the day. That was the last time he had felt this, this sense of being a burden to all. Two years since he had proved too much for even a rope to bear.

It was a poor knot he had tied. Morgan would've been disgusted by the effort. But his hands had been trembling and he had fought to see the knot through a film of tears. When it failed, the knot didn't come free so much as slide, and it left his neck afire and bleeding. His great regret was having jumped from the lower stairwell in Mechanical, the rope looped over the pipes above. If he had gone from a landing, the slipping knot wouldn't have mattered. The fall would've claimed him.

Now he was too scared to try again. He was as scared of trying again as he was of being a burden to another. Was that why he avoided seeing Allie, because she longed to care for him? To help support him? Was that why he ran away from home? Why he pined for a girl that he knew deep down cared more for another?

The intolerableness grew until Mission began to hate the boy stuffed in that bag with him. A boy too scared to live, too frightened to die.

The tears finally came. His arms were pinned, so he couldn't wipe them away. He thought of his mother, about whom he could only piece together a few details. But he knew this of her: She hadn't been afraid of life or death. She had embraced both in an act that he knew he would never make worthy.

More tears. And there weren't enough chits in the silo to pay back the debt of being carried by others. The silo spun slowly around him; the steps sank one at a time; and Mission endured the suffering of this self-discovery. He labored not to sob, seeing himself for the first time in that utter darkness, knowing his soul more fully in that deathly ritual of being ported to his grave, this sad awakening on his birthday.

• Silo 1 •

Fear cannot be without hope nor hope without fear.

-Baruch Spinoza

·27·

Finding one among ten thousand should've been more difficult than this. It should've taken months of crawling through reports and databases, of querying the Head of 18 and asking for personality profiles, of looking at arrest histories, cleaning schedules, who was related to whom, where people spent their time, and all the gossip and chatter compiled from monthly reports.

But Donald found an easier way. He simply searched the database for *himself*.

One who remembers. One full of fear and paranoia. One who tries to blend in but is subversive. He looked for a fear of doctors, teasing out those residents who never went to see them. He looked for someone who shunned medication and found one who did not even trust the water. A part of him expected he might find several people to be causing so much havoc, a pack, and that locating one among them would lead to the rest. He expected to find them young and outraged with some way of handing down what they knew from generation to generation.

This was what he expected, and so he put it out of mind. He did not act on what was probable. He stayed up for most of the night searching simply for himself. He searched for himself the way he had searched for Helen and his sister. And what he found was both eerily similar and not like him at all.

The next morning, he showed his results to Thurman, who stood perfectly still for a long while.

"Of course," he finally said. He looked at Anna, his daughter, with tears in his eyes. "Of course."

A hand on Donald's shoulder was all the congratulations he got. Thurman explained that the reset was well underway. He admitted that it had been underway since Donald had been woken. Erskine and Dr. Henson were working through the night to make changes, to come up with a new formulation, but this component might take weeks. Looking over what Donald had found, he said he was going to make a call to 18.

"I want to come with you," Donald said. "It's my theory."

What he wanted to say was that he wouldn't take the coward's way. If someone was to be executed on his account—a life taken in order to save others—he didn't want to remove himself, to hide from it.

Thurman agreed.

They rode the lift almost as equals. Donald asked why Thurman had started the reset, but he thought he knew the answer.

"Vic won," was Thurman's reply.

Donald thought of the lives in a database that were now thrown into chaos. This is what generals and politicians felt, sitting in a room some comfortable distance away, gathered around a table where death was planned and hoped against. He made the mistake of asking how the reset was going, and Thurman told him about the bombs and the recruits, how these things typically went, that the recipe was as old as time.

"The combustibles are always there," he said. "You'd be surprised at how few sparks it takes."

They exited the lift and walked down a familiar hallway. This was Donald's old commute. Here, he had worked under a different name. He had worked without knowing what he was doing. They passed offices full of people clacking on keyboards and chatting with one another. Half a millennium of people coming on and off shifts, doing what they were told, following orders.

He couldn't help himself as they approached his old office: he paused at the door and peered in. A thin man with a halo of hair that wrapped from ear to ear, just a few wisps on top, looked up at him. He sat there, mouth agape, hand resting on his mouse, waiting for Donald to say or do something.

Donald nodded a sympathetic hello. He turned and looked through the door across the hall where a man in white sat behind a similar desk. The puppeteer. It was a wonder people didn't trip on the strings.

Thurman spoke to the man in white, who got up from his desk and joined them in the hall. Here was one who seemed to know that Thurman was in charge. Tiers of puppets.

Donald followed the two of them to the comm room, leaving the balding man at his old desk to his game of solitaire. He felt a mix of sympathy and envy for the man, this captain at a rudderless wheel. Sympathy and envy for those who don't remember. As they turned the corner, Donald thought back to those initial bouts of awareness on his first shift. He remembered speaking with a doctor who knew, and having this sense of wonder that anyone could cope with such knowledge. And now he saw that it wasn't that the pain grew tolerable or the confusion went away. Instead, it simply became familiar. It became a part of you. It was a nasty scar that still flared up now and then but that you lived with.

The comm room was quiet. Heads swiveled as the three of them entered. One of the operators hurriedly removed his feet from his desk. Another took a bite of his protein bar and turned back to his station.

"Get me Eighteen," Thurman said.

Eyes turned to the other man in white, who waved his consent. A call was patched through. Thurman held half a headset to one ear while he waited. He caught the expression on Donald's face and waved the operator for another set. Donald stepped forward and accepted it while the cable was slotted into the receiver. He could hear the familiar beeping of a call being placed, and his stomach fluttered as doubts began to surface. Finally, a voice answered. A shadow.

Thurman asked him to get Mr. Wyck, the silo Head.

"He's already coming," the shadow said.

When Wyck joined the conversation, Thurman told the Head what Donald had found, but it was the shadow who responded. The shadow knew the one they were after. He said that they were close. There was something in his voice, some shock or hesitation, and Thurman waved at the operator to get the sensors in his headset going. Suddenly, it was a Rite of Initiation they were conducting. This shadow became Thurman's target, and Donald watched a master at work.

"Tell me what you know," he said. Thurman leaned over the operator and peered at a screen that monitored skin conductivity, heartbeat, and perspiration. Donald was no expert at reading the charts, but he knew something was up by the way the lines spiked up and down while the shadow spoke. He feared for the young man. He wondered if someone would die then and there.

But such was not Thurman's intent. Within moments, he had the boy speaking of his childhood, had him admitting to this rage he harbored, a sense of not belonging, the need to act up and lash out. He spoke of a childhood that seemed both ideal and frustrating, and Thurman was like a gentle but firm drill sergeant working with a troubled recruit: tearing him down, building him back up.

"You've been fed the truth," he told the young man. "And now you see why it must be divvied out carefully or not at all."

"I do."

The shadow sniffed as though he were crying. And yet: the jagged lines on the screen formed less precipitous peaks, less dangerous valleys.

Thurman spoke of sacrifice, of the greater good, of individual lives proving meaningless in the far stretch of time. He took that shadow's rage and redirected it until the work of being locked up for months with the Legacy was distilled down to its very essence. And through it all, it didn't sound as though the silo Head breathed once.

"Tell me what needs to be fixed," Thurman said, after their discussion. He laid the problem at the shadow's feet. Donald saw how this was better than simply handing him the solution.

The shadow spoke of a culture forming that overvalued individuality, of children that wanted to get away from their families, of generations living levels apart and independence stressed until no one relied on anyone and everyone was dispensable.

The sobs came. Donald watched as Thurman's face tightened, and he wondered again if he was about to see a death ordered, a young man put out of his misery. Instead, the white-haired general, this senator of another time, released the radio for a moment and said to those gathered around, simply, "He's ready."

And what started as an inquiry, a test of Donald's theory, concluded this boy's dose of the Legacy and his Rite of Initiation. A shadow became a man. Lines on a screen settled into steel cords of resolve as his anger was given a new focus, a new purpose. His childhood was seen differently. Dangerously.

Thurman gave this young man his first order. Mr. Wyck congratulated the boy and provided his freedom. And later, as Donald and Thurman rode the elevator back toward Anna, Thurman declared that this Rodny would make a fine silo Head. Even better than the last.

·28·

That afternoon, Donald and Anna worked to restore order to the war room. They made it ready in case it was called upon during a future shift. All their notes were taken off the walls and filed away into airtight plastic crates, and Donald imagined these would sit on another level somewhere, another storeroom, to gather dust. The computers were unplugged, all the wiring coiled up, and these were hauled off by Erskine on a cart with squeaky wheels. All that was left were the cots, a change of clothes, and the standard issue toiletries. Enough to get them through the night and to their meeting with Dr. Henson the following day.

Several shifts were about to come to a close. For Anna and Thurman, it had been a long time coming. Two full shifts. Almost a year awake. Erskine and Henson would need a few weeks to finish their work, and by that time the next Head would come on, and the schedule would return to normal. For Donald, it had been less than a week awake after nearly a century of sleep. He was a dead man who had blinked his eyes open for but a moment. Just a peek, and now back again.

Something told him his dreams would be different this time. There might still be a mountain of skulls to climb, but some of those bleached skulls with their empty sockets would now have names. Names gleaned from a database. Families that may or may not survive the great reset of Silo 18. Some that would die so that others might live.

He thought of them as he took his last shower, as he brushed his teeth, took his first dose of the bitter drink so that no one would think anything was amiss. But Donald didn't plan on sleeping or dreaming. To him, this deep freeze was worse than death. Not only did it carry him farther and farther from Helen, whisking him through the years while she returned to dust, the deep freeze was a false sleep that could only be filled with nightmares and only be disturbed by tragedy.

If he went back to sleep, they would never get him up again. He knew that. Unless things were so bad that he wouldn't want to be woken anyway. Unless it were Anna once more, lonely, wishing for company, and willing to subject him to abuse in order to get it.

That wasn't sleep. That was a body and a mind stored away. There were other choices, more final ways out. Donald had discovered this resolve by following a trail of clues left behind by Victor, and he would soon arrive at the man's same fateful conclusion.

He walked a final lap amid the guns and drones. He touched the wings beneath the tarps, and finally retired to his cot. He thought of Helen as he lay there listening to Anna sing in the shower one last time. And he realized the anger he had felt for his wife having lived and loved without him was now gone. It had been wiped away by his guilt for coming to find solace in Anna's embrace. And when she came to him that night, straight from the shower with water beading on her flesh, he could not be strong. They had the same bitter drink on their breath, that concoction that prepped their veins for the deep sleep, and neither of them cared. Donald succumbed. And then he waited until she had returned to her cot and her breathing had softened before he cried himself to sleep. And in that sleep, he discovered no doubts about the voyage he had planned for the following day.

When he woke, Anna was already gone, her cot neatly made. Donald did the same, tucking the sheets beneath the mattress and leaving the corners crisp, even though he knew the sheets would be mussed as the cots were returned to their rightful place in the barracks. He checked the time. Anna had been put under during the early morning so as not to be spotted. He had less than an hour before Thurman would come for him. It was more than enough time.

He went out to the storeroom and approached the drone nearest the hangar door. Yanking the tarp off sent a cloud of dust into the air. Donald coughed and covered his mouth. He waved his hand in the air, then dragged out the empty bin he had stuffed under one of the wings. He opened the low hangar door and arranged the tough plastic bin so that it was slightly inside the lift. He lowered the door onto the bin to keep the small hangar propped open.

Opening the adjacent door, he hurried down the hallway, past the empty barracks, and pulled the plastic sheet off the station at the very end. His explorations had recently turned from discovery into experimentation. Flipping the plastic cover off the lift switch, he threw it into the up position. The first time he'd done this, the door to the lift would no longer open, but he could hear the platform rumbling upward on the other side of the wall. It hadn't taken long to figure out a solution.

Replacing the plastic sheet, he hurried down the hall. He could still taste the bitter prepping agent in his mouth and wished he'd been able to avoid drinking that. It would be a horrible final taste.

He turned off the light in the hall and shut the door. The other bin was pulled out from under the drone's left wing. The contents had been assembled and arranged carefully. Donald stripped and tossed his clothes under the drone. He pulled out the thick plastic suit and sat down to work his feet into the legs. The boots went on next, Donald being careful to seal the cuffs around them. Standing up, he gripped the dangling shoelace stolen from an extra boot. The end had been tied to the zipper on the back of the suit. He pulled it over his shoulder and tugged upward, hand over hand, like he'd seen surfers and divers do. He made sure the zipper went to the top before pulling the gloves, flashlight, and helmet from the bin.

The helmet went on before the gloves, as the latches were difficult to operate. After tugging on the second glove, he did one final check of the suit to be sure everything was properly sealed. Satisfied, he closed the bin and slid the container back under the wing before covering the drone with the tarp. There would only be a single trunk out of place when Thurman arrived. Victor had left a mess to discover. Donald would hardly leave a trace.

He crawled inside the lift on his belly, pushing the flashlight ahead of him. He could hear the motor inside straining against the pinned bin to move upward, a whirring like an angry hive of bees. Turning on the flashlight, he took a last look at the storeroom, braced himself, then kicked the plastic tub with both boots.

It budged. There was a scraping sound. He kicked again, and the lift shook from the violence. Just a few more inches. A last kick, and he barely got his boots back inside in time. There was a thunderous racket as the door slammed shut, a bang like an explosion, and then he felt the shudder of movement. Cables rattled and sang above. The flashlight jittered and danced. Donald corralled the loose flashlight between his mitts and watched his exhalations fog the inside of his helmet. He had no idea what to expect, but he was causing it. For once, he was the agent of change. He was going somewhere by choice.

·29·

The ride up took much longer than he anticipated. There were moments when he wasn't sure whether or not he was still moving. His body told him several times that he was in fact heading back down, that he had changed direction. He grew worried that his plan had been discovered, that the misplaced bin had led them to his tracks in the dust, that he was being recalled. He urged the lift to hurry along.

His flashlight gave out. Donald tapped the cylinder in his mitt and worked the switch back and forth. It must've been on a weak charge from its long storage. He was left in the dark with all the sensation of a man beneath the sea on a moonless night, no way of knowing which way was up nor down, whether he was bobbing or sinking, rising or drowning. All he could do was wait. And again, he knew that this was the right decision. There was nothing worse than being trapped in the darkness, unable to do anything more than wait. This final time would mark the end of his suffering.

Arrival came with a jarring clank. The persistent hum of the motor disappeared, the ensuing quiet haunting. There was a second clank, and then the door opposite the one he'd entered slowly rose. A metal nub on the floor the size of a fist slid forward on a track that linked up with a groove outside. Donald scrambled after this nub, seeing how the drone might be guided forward.

He found himself in a sloping launch bay. He hadn't known what to expect, thought maybe he'd simply arrive above the soil on a barren landscape, but he was in a shaft. A dim light grew stronger. Above him, up the slope, a slit was opening. Beyond this slit, Donald spotted the roiling clouds he knew from the cafe. They were the bright gray that came with a sunrise. The doors at the top of the slope continued to slide apart like a maw opening wide.

Donald crawled up the steep slope as quickly as he could. The metal car in the track stopped and locked into place. Donald hurried, imagining he didn't have much time. He stayed off the track in case the launch sequence was automated, but the nub never moved, never raced by. He arrived at the open doors exhausted and perspiring and managed to haul himself out.

The world spread out before him. After a week of living in a windowless chamber and decades of sleeping in a virtual grave, the scale and openness were inspiring. Donald felt like tearing off his helmet and sucking in deep breaths of non-confinement. The oppressive weight of his silo imprisonment had been lifted. Above him were only the clouds.

He stood on a round concrete platform. Behind the opening for the launch ramp was a cluster of antennas. He went to these, held onto one of them, and lowered himself to the wide ledge below. From here it was a scramble on his belly, trying to hold onto the slick edge with bulky gloves, and then a graceless drop to the dirt.

He scanned the horizon for the city—had to work his way around the tower to find it. From there, he aimed forty-five degrees to the left. He had studied the maps to make sure, but now that he was there, he realized he could've done it by memory. Over there was where the tents had stood, and here the stage, and beyond them the dirt tracks through the struggling beginnings of grass as ATVs buzzed up the hillside. He could almost smell the food that'd been cooking, could hear the dogs barking and children playing, the anthems in the air.

Donald shook off thoughts of the past and made his time count. He knew there was a chance—a very good chance—that someone was sitting at breakfast in the cafe. They would be dropping their spoon into their reconstituted eggs right then and pointing at the wallscreen. But he had a head start. They would have to wrestle with suits and wonder if the risk was worth it. By the time they got to him, it would be too late. Hopefully, they would simply leave him.

He worked his way up the hillside. Movement was a struggle inside the bulky suit. He slipped and fell several times in the slick soil. When a gust of wind hammered the landscape, it peppered his helmet with grit and made a noise like the hiss of Anna's radio. There was no telling how long the suit would last. He knew enough of the cleaning to suspect it wouldn't be forever, but Anna had told him that the machines in the air were designed to attack only certain things. That was why they didn't destroy the sensors, or the concrete, or a proper suit. And he suspected his silo would only have proper suits.

All he hoped for as he labored up the hill was a view. He was so obsessed and determined to win this that he never thought to look behind him. Always ahead. Slipping and scrambling, crawling on his hands and knees the last fifty feet, until finally he was at the summit. He stood and staggered forward, exhausted, breathing heavily, remembering the bombs in the air and Anna pulling him back to safety, back to hell.

Not this time. He reached the edge and looked down into the adjacent bowl. There, a concrete tower stood like a gravestone, like a monument to Helen. She was buried below, and while he could never go to her, never be buried alongside her, he could lie down beneath the clouds and be close enough.

He wanted his helmet off. First, though, his gloves. He tugged one of them free—popping the seal—and dropped it to the soil. The heavy winds, heavy enough that he found himself leaning into them, sent the glove tumbling down the slope. The grit in the heavy breeze stung his hand. The peppering of fine particles burned like a day on a windy beach. Donald began tugging on his other glove, resigned to what would come next, when suddenly he felt a hand grip his shoulder, and he was yanked back from the edge of that gentle rise, that hard-fought and pleasant view.

·30·

Donald stumbled and fell. The shock of being touched sent his heart into his throat. He waved his arms to free himself, but someone had a grip on his suit. More than one person. They dragged him back until he could no longer see Helen's resting spot.

His screams of frustration filled his helmet. Couldn't they see that it was too late? Couldn't they leave him be? He flailed and tried to lunge out of their grip, but he was being pulled down the hill, back toward Silo 1.

When he fell the next time, he was able to roll over and face them, to get his arms up to fend for himself. And there was Thurman standing over him—wearing nothing more than his white coveralls. Dust from the dead earth gathered in the old man's gray brow.

"It's time to go!" Thurman yelled into the heavy wind. His voice seemed as distant as the clouds.

Donald kicked his feet and tried to move like a crab back up the hill, but there were three of them there. All in white, squinting against the ferocity of the driving wind and pelting soil. And they were, none of them, pleased.

"Nooo!" Donald yelled, as they seized him again. He tried to grab rocks and fistfuls of soil as they pulled him along by his boots. His helmet knocked against the lifeless pack of dirt. He watched the clouds boil overhead as his fingernails were bent back and broken in his struggle for some purchase.

By the time they got him to the flats, Donald was spent. They carried him down a ramp and through the airlock where more men were waiting. His helmet was tossed aside before the outer door fully shut. Thurman stood in a far corner and watched as they undressed him. The old man dabbed at the blood running from his nose. Donald had caught him with his boot.

Erskine was there, Dr. Henson as well, both of them breathing hard. As soon as they got his suit off, Henson plunged a needle into Donald's flesh. Erskine held his hand and seemed sad. A darkness like death spread through Donald's veins.

"A bloody waste," someone said, as the fog settled over him.

"Look at this mess."

Erskine placed a hand on Donald's cheek as Donald drifted deeper into the black. His lids grew heavy and his hearing distant.

"Be better if someone like you were in charge," he heard Erskine say.

But it was Victor's voice he heard. It was a dream. No, a memory. A thought from an earlier conversation. Donald couldn't be sure. The waking world of boots and angry voices was too busy being swallowed by the mist of sleep and the fog of dreams. And this time—rather than with a fear of death—Donald went into that darkness gladly. He embraced it hoping it would be eternal. He went with a final thought of his sister, of those drones beneath their tarps, and all that he hoped would never be woken.

• Silo 18 •

Ring around the silo.
No one knows what I know.
Ashes! Ashes! We all fall down!

·31·

Mission felt buried alive. He fell into an uncomfortable trance, the bag growing hot and slick as it trapped his heat and exhalations. Part of him feared he would pass out in there and Joel and Lyn would discover him dead. Part of him hoped.

The two porters were stopped for questioning on one-seventeen, a landing below the blast that took Cam. Those working to repair the stairwell were on the lookout for a certain porter. Their description was part Cam, part Mission. Mission held deathly still while Joel complained of being stopped with so sensitive and heavy a load. It seemed that they might demand the bag be opened, but there were some things nearly as taboo as talk of the outside. And so they were let free with a warning that the rail was out above and that one person had already fallen to their death.

Mission fought off a coughing fit as the voices receded below. He wiggled his shoulders and struggled to cover his mouth to muffle the sound of his throat being cleared. Lyn hissed at him to be quiet. In the distance, Mission could hear a woman wailing. They passed through the wreckage from hours earlier, and Joel and Lyn gasped at the sight of an entire landing torn free from the stairwell.

Above Supply, they carried him into a restroom, opened the bag, and let him work the blood back into his arms. Mission peed and took a few sips of water. He assured the others that he was fine in there. Yes, it was hot, he told them. All three of them were damp with sweat, and there was a very long way to go. Joel especially seemed weary from the levels climbed thus far, or perhaps from seeing the damage wreaked by the blast. Lyn was holding up better but was anxious to get going again. She fretted aloud for Rodny and seemed as eager to get to the Nest as Mission.

Mission looked at himself in the mirror with his white coveralls and his porter's knife strapped to his waist. He was the one they were looking for. He drew his knife and held a handful of his hair. It made a crunching noise, like biting into celery, as he sawed through a clump close to his scalp. Lyn saw what he was doing and helped with her own knife. It hurt in a good way and made his head tingle. Joel grabbed the trashcan from the corner to collect the hair.

It was a rough job, but he looked less like the one they wanted. Before putting his knife away, he cut a few slits in the black bag, right by the zipper. He peeled off his undershirt and wiped the inside of the bag dry before throwing the shirt in the trashcan. It reeked of smoke and sweat, anyway. Crawling back inside, helping with the straps, they zipped him up and carried him back to the stairway to resume their ascent. Mission was powerless to do anything but worry.

He ran over the events of a very long day. Things had happened that morning that felt like they must've taken place yesterday. He remembered getting up early to watch the clouds brighten over breakfast. He had visited the Crow and delivered her note, had then lost a friend, and now was heading back to the Nest. The exhaustion of it all caught up to him. Or perhaps it was the lack of sleep from the fight the night before or the gentle swaying of the bag. Whatever the cause, he found himself sliding into unconsciousness.

He didn't sleep so much as cease to be for a while. Time marched along without him.

When he startled awake, it felt but a moment later. His coveralls were damp, the inside of the bag slick again with condensation. Joel must've felt him jerk to consciousness, as he quickly shushed Mission and told him they were coming up on Central.

Mission's heart pounded as he came to and remembered where he was, what they were doing. It felt difficult to breathe. The slits he had cut were lost in the folds of the plastic. He wanted the zipper cracked, just a slice of light, a whisper of fresh air. His arms were pinned and numb from the straps around his shoulders. His ankles were sore from where Lyn was hoisting him from below.

"Can't breathe," he gasped.

The others shushed him. But there was a pause, an end to the swaying. Someone fumbled with the bag over his head, a series of tiny clicks from a zipper lowering a dozen notches.

Mission sucked in cool gasps. The world resumed its swaying, boots striking the stairs in the distance—a commotion somewhere above or below, he couldn't tell. More fighting. More dying. He saw bodies spinning through the air. He saw Cam leaving the farm sublevels just the day before, a coroner's bonus in his pocket, no thought of how little time he had left for spending it. No thought from any of them how little time they had left to spend anything.

They rested at Central Dispatch. Mission was let out in the main hallway, which was frighteningly empty. "What the hell happened here?" Lyn asked. She dug her finger into a hole in the wall surrounded by a spiderweb of cracks. There were hundreds of holes like them. Boots rang on the landing and continued past.

"What time is it?" Mission asked, keeping his voice down.

"It's after dinner," Joel said. It meant they were making good time.

Down the hall, Lyn studied a dark patch of what looked to be rust. "Is this blood?" she hissed.

"Robbie said he couldn't reach anyone down here," Mission said. "Maybe they scattered."

Joel took a sip from his canteen. "Or were driven off." He wiped his mouth with his sleeve.

"Should we stay here for the night? You two look beat."

Joel frowned and shook his head. He offered Mission his canteen. "I think we need to get past the thirties. Security is everywhere. Hell, you could probably dash up with what you've got on the way they're running about. Might need to clean up your hair a bit."

Mission rubbed his scalp and thought about that. "Maybe I should," he said. "I could be up there before the dim-time." He watched as Lyn disappeared into one of the bunk rooms down the hall. She emerged almost immediately with her hand over her mouth, her eyes wide.

"What is it?" Mission asked, pushing up from a crouch and joining her.

She threw her arms around him and held him away from the door, buried her face into his shoulder. Joel risked a look.

"No," he whispered.

Mission pulled away from Lyn and joined his fellow porter by the door.

The bunks were full. Some lay sprawled on the floor, but it was obvious by the tangle of their limbs—the way arms hung useless from bunks or were twisted beneath them—that these porters weren't sleeping.

They discovered Katelyn among them. None of them could abide seeing her like that, which cemented Mission's plan to dash up on his own. Lyn shook with silent sobs as he and Joel retrieved Katelyn's body and loaded her into the bag. Mission felt a pang of guilt to think that it was nice how small Katelyn was. Awful porter thoughts.

They were securing the straps and zipping her up when the power in the hallway went out, leaving them in the pitch black. They groped for one another, even the light spilling through the doors leading out onto the landing suddenly gone.

"What the hell?" Joel hissed.

A moment later, the lights returned but flickered as though an unsteady flame burned in each bulb. Mission wiped the sweat from his forehead and wished he still had his 'chief.

"If you can't make it all the way tonight," he said to the others, "stop and stay at the waystation and check on Robbie."

"We'll be fine," Joel assured him.

Lyn squeezed his arm before he went. "Watch your steps," she said.

"And you," Mission told them.

He hurried toward the landing and the great stairway beyond. Overhead, the lights flickered like little flames. A sign that something, somewhere, perhaps was burning.

·32·

He hurried upward amid a fog of smoke and rumor, and Mission's throat burned from the one, his mind from the other. An explosion in Mechanical was whispered to have been the reason for the blackout. Talk swirled of a bent or broken shaft and that the silo was on backup power. He heard such things from half a spiral away as he took the steps two and sometimes three at a time. It felt good to be out and moving, good to have his muscles aching rather than sitting still, to be his own burden.

And he noticed that when anyone saw him, they either fell silent or scattered beyond their landings, even those he knew. At first, he feared it was from recognition. But it was the Security white he wore. Young men just like him thundered up and down the stairwell terrorizing everyone. They were yesterday's farmers, welders, and pumpmen—and they brought order with their strange and dark weapons.

More than once, a group of them stopped Mission and asked where he was going, where his rifle was. He told them that he had been a part of the fighting below and was reporting back. It was something he'd heard another claim. Many of them seemed to know as little as he did, and so they would let him pass. As ever, the color you wore said everything. People could know you at a glance.

The activity grew thicker near IT. A group of new recruits passed, and Mission watched over the railing as they kicked in the doors to the level below and stormed inside. People screamed. There was a sharp bang like a heavy steel rod falling to the steel decking. A dozen of these bangs, and then less screaming. Fear was in everyone's eyes, no less those in white who seemed to know as little of what they were doing as Mission. Just chaos like a switch had been thrown. A steady pulse of light one day, and now the faltering of a dying flame.

He passed IT, the doors closed, and thought for a moment about barging in and trying to talk his way past the guards. But not alone. Tomorrow, with his friends.

His legs were sore, a stitch in his side, as he approached the farms. He caught sight of Winters and a few others out on the landing with shovels and rakes. Someone yelled something as he passed. Mission quickened his pace, thinking of his father and brother, seeing the wisdom for once in his old man's unwillingness to leave that patch of dirt.

A bag of berries on the stairwell looked at first like a blood stain. They had been stepped on and crushed, but Mission picked up the bag anyway. He scooped the mush out with his fingers as he hurried on, grateful for the find. He left the empty bag on the next landing, remembering days when such plastic was filled with paint and dropped on others. Those no longer seemed like the good times.

After a lifetime of racing up with the smoke as his company, of rising with the drifting ash, he reached the quiet of the Nest.

The little chicks were gone. Most people were probably holed up in their apartments, families cowering together, hoping this madness would pass like others had. Inside, several lockers stood open. A child's backpack lay in the middle of the hall. Mission staggered forward on numb legs toward the sound of a familiar singing voice and the screech of something awful.

At the end of the hall, her door stood as welcome and open as always. The singing was from the Crow, whose voice seemed stronger than usual. Mission saw that he wasn't the first to arrive, that his wire had gone out. Frankie and Allie were there, both in the green and white of farm security. They were arranging desks while Mrs. Crowe sang. The sheets had been thrown off the stacks of desks kept in storage along one wall. Those desks now filled the classroom the way Mission remembered from his youth. It was as though the Crow was expecting them to be filled at any time.

Allie noticed him first. She rushed over, her coveralls bunched up around her boots, the straps knotted to make them shorter. They must've been Frankie's coveralls. As she threw herself into his arms, he wondered what the two of them had risked to meet him there.

"Mission, my boy." Mrs. Crowe stopped her singing, smiled, and waved him over. After a moment, Allie reluctantly loosened her grip.

Mission shook Frankie's hand and thanked him for coming. It took a moment to realize something was different, that his hair had been cut short as well. They both rubbed their scalps and laughed. Humor came easy in humorless times.

"What is this I hear about my Rodny?" the Crow asked him. Her chair twitched back and forth, her hand working the controls, her Thursday dress tucked under her narrow bones. Mission drew a deep breath, smoke lingering in his lungs, and he began to tell them all he had seen on the stairwell, about the bombs and the fires and what he had heard of Mechanical, the Security forces with their barking rifles like the dogs of Supply—but the Crow dispelled his frenzied chatter with a wave of her frail arms.

"Not the fighting," she said. "The fighting I've seen. I could paint a picture of the fighting and hang it from my walls. What of Rodny? What of our boy? Has he got them?" She made a small fist and held it aloft.

"No," Mission said. "He needs our help."

The Crow laughed, which took him aback. He tried to explain. "I gave him your note, and he passed me one in return. It begged for help. They have him locked up behind these great steel doors—"

"Not locked up," the Crow said.

"—like he'd done something wrong—"

"Something *right*," she said, correcting him.

Mission fell silent. He could see knowledge shining behind her old eyes, a sunrise on the day after a cleaning.

"Rodny is in no danger," she said.

Allie squeezed Mission's arm. "She's been trying to tell us," she whispered. "Everything's going to be okay. Come, help with the desks."

"But the note," Mission said, wishing he hadn't turned it to confetti.

"The note you gave him was to give him strength. To let him know it was time to begin." There was a wildness in the Crow's eyes, excitement and joy becoming something more combustible than either.

"No," Mission said. "Rodny was afraid. I know my friend, and he was afraid of something."

The Crow's face hardened. She relaxed her fist and smoothed the front of her faded dress. "If that be the case," she said, her voice trembling. "Then I judged him most wrongly."

·33·

The dim-time approached while they arranged desks and the Crow resumed her singing. Allie told him a curfew had been announced, and so Mission lost hope that the others would show up that night. They pulled out mats from the cubbies to rest, plan, and give the others until daybreak. There was much Mission wanted to ask the Crow, but she seemed distracted, her thoughts elsewhere, a joyousness that made her giddy.

Frankie felt certain he could get them through security and deeper into IT if only he could reach his father. Mission told them how well he'd been able to move about with the whites on. Maybe he could reach Frankie's dad in a pinch. Allie produced fresh fruits harvested from her plot and passed them around. The Crow drank one of her dark green concoctions. Mission grew restless.

He wandered out to the landing, torn between waiting for the others and his anxiety to get going. For all he knew, Rodny was being marched up to his death already. Cleanings tended to settle people down, to come after bouts of unrest, but this was unlike any of the spates of violence he had seen before. This was the burning his father spoke of, the embers of distrust and crumbling trade that jumped up all at once. He had seen this coming, but it had approached with the swiftness of a knife plummeting from the Up Top.

Out on the landing, he heard the sounds of a mob echoing from far below. Holding the landing rail, he could feel the hum of many marching boots. He returned to the others and said nothing of it. There was no reason to suspect those boots were marching for them.

Allie looked as though she'd been crying when he got back. Her eyes were moist, her cheeks flushed. The Crow was telling them an Old Time story, her hands painting a scene in the air. Mission asked Allie if everything was all right.

She shook her head like she'd rather not say.

"What is it?" he asked. He held her hand, heard the Crow speaking of Atlantis, another tale of the crumbling and lost city of magic beyond the hills, a bygone day when those ruins shone like a wet dime.

"Tell me," he said. He wondered if maybe those stories were affecting her the way they sometimes did him, making her sad and not knowing why.

"I didn't want to say anything until after," she cried, fresh tears welling up. She wiped them away, and the Crow fell silent, her hands falling to her lap. Frankie sat quietly. Whatever it was, the two of them knew as well.

"Father," Mission said. It had to do with his father. Allie was close to his father in a way that Mission had never been. And suddenly, he felt a powerful regret for ever having left home. While she wiped her eyes, the words unable to form on her trembling lips, Mission imagined himself on his hands and knees, in the dirt, digging for forgiveness. He thought of growing corn rather than hauling it. Of making something rather than being paid a chit for rumors that ought to be free.

Allie bawled, and the Crow hummed a tune of aboveground days. Mission thought of his father, gone, all he longed to say, and wanted nothing more than to hurl himself at the posters on the walls, to tear them down and rip to shreds their urgings to go and be free.

"It's Riley," Allie finally said. "Mish, I'm so sorry."

The Crow ceased her humming. All three of them watched him.

"No," Mission whispered.

"You shouldn't have told him—" Frankie began.

"He ought to know!" Allie demanded. "He's an only son, now. His father would want him to know."

Mission gazed at a poster of green hills and blue skies. That world blurred with tears as surely as it might with dust. "What happened?" he whispered.

She told him that there'd been an attack on the farms. Riley had begged to go and help fight, had been told no, and then disappeared. He'd been found with a knife from the kitchen still clutched in his hands.

Mission stood and paced the room, tears splashing from his cheeks. He shouldn't have gone. Ever. He should've been there. He wasn't there for Cam, either. Death preceded him in all the places he couldn't be. He had done the same to his mother. And now the end was coming for them all.

There was someone in the hallway. Mission wiped his cheeks. He had given up on any of the others coming and thought it might be Security with their guns, instead. They would ask him where his own gun was before realizing he was an impostor, before shooting them all. He thought about Jenine, had the sickening feeling that his call to arms had placed others in danger. More deathdays.

He pushed the door shut, saw that the Crow had no lock on the thing, and wedged a desk under the handle. Frankie grabbed another desk. Mission didn't see that they would do any good. He hurried toward Allie, told her to get behind the Crow's desk. He grabbed the back of the old teacher's wheelchair—the overhead wire swinging dangerously—but she insisted she could manage herself, that there was nothing to be afraid of.

Mission knew better. This was Security coming for them—Security or some other mob. He'd traveled the stairwell, knew what was out there. This was something bad coming, not his friends. There was no part of him that thought it might be *both*.

There was a knock on the door. The handle jiggled. The boots outside quieted as they gathered around. Frankie pressed his finger to his lips, his eyes wide. The wire overhead creaked as it swung back and forth.

The door budged. Mission hoped for a moment that they would go away, that they were just making their rounds. He thought about hiding under the sheets used to cover the unneeded desks, but the thought came too late. The door was shoved open, a desk crying as it skittered across the floor, and the first person through was Rodny.

His sudden appearance was as jarring as a bomb. He wore white coveralls, the creases still in them like a great letter H across his stomach and down his chest. His hair had been cut short, his face newly shaved, a nick on his chin.

Mission felt as though he were staring into a mirror, the two of them in costume, the same costume. More men in white crowded behind Rodny in the hallway, rifles in hand. Rodny ordered them back and stepped into the room where all those tiny desks lay neatly arranged and empty.

Allie was the first to respond. She gasped with surprise and hurried forward, arms wide as if for an embrace. Rodny held up a palm and told her to stop. His other hand held a small gun like the deputies wore. His eyes were not on his friends but on the Old Crow.

"Rodny—" Mission began. His brain attempted to grasp his friend's presence. They were there to go rescue him, but he looked in little need of it.

"The door," Rodny said over his shoulder.

A man twice Rodny's age hesitated before doing as he was asked and pulling the door shut. This was not the demeanor of a prisoner. It was one who held captive the attention of others. Frankie lurched forward before the door shut all the way, calling "Father," as he caught a glimpse of his old man in the hall with the others.

"We were coming for you," Mission said. He wanted to approach his friend, but there was something dangerous in Rodny's eyes. "Your note—"

Rodny finally looked away from the Crow.

"We were coming to help—" Mission said.

"Yesterday, I needed it," Rodny said. He circled around the desks, the gun at his side, his eyes flicking from face to face. Mission backed up and joined Allie in standing close to the Crow, whether to protect her or feel protected, he couldn't say.

"You shouldn't be here," Mrs. Crowe said with a lecturing tone. "This is not where your fight is."

The gun rose a little.

"What're you doing?" Allie asked of her old friend.

Rodny pointed at the Crow. "Tell them," he said. "Tell them what you've done. What you do."

"What've they done to you?" Mission asked. His friend was different beyond the garb.

"They showed me—" Rodny swept his gun at the posters on the wall. "That these stories are true." He laughed and turned to the Crow. "And I was angry, just like you said. Angry at what they did to the world."

"So hurt them," the Crow insisted, her voice creaking like a door about to slam.

"But now I know. They told me. We got a call. And now I know what you've been doing here—"

"What's this about?" Frankie asked, still in the middle of the room. He moved toward the door. "Why is my father—?"

"Stay," Rodny told him. He pushed one of the desks out of the way and moved down the aisle. "Don't you move." His gun swung from Frankie to the Crow, whose chair shivered in time with her palsied hand. "These sayings on the wall, the stories and songs, you made us what we are. You made us angry."

"You should be," she screeched. "You damn well should be!"

Mission moved closer to her. He kept his eye on the gun. Allie knelt and held the old woman's hand. Rodny stood ten paces away, the gun angled at their feet.

"They kill and they kill," the Crow said. "And this will go the way it always has. Wipe it all clean. Bury and burn the dead. And these desks—" Her arm shot up, her quivering finger aimed at the empty desks newly arranged. "These desks will be *full* again."

"No," Rodny said. He shook his head. "No more. It ends here. You won't terrify us anymore—"

"What're you saying?" Mission asked. He stepped close to the

Crow, a hand on her chair. "You're the one with the gun, Rodny. You're the one scaring us."

Rodny turned toward Mission. "*She* makes us feel this way. Don't you see? The fear and hope go hand in hand. What she sells is no different than the priests, only she gets to us *first*. This talk of a better world. It just makes us hate *this* one."

"No—" Mission hated his friend for uttering such a thing.

"Yes," Rodny said. "Why do you think we hate our fathers? It's because her stories are true. But this won't make it better." He waved his hand. "Not that it matters. What I knew yesterday had me terrified for my life. For all of us. What I know now gives me hope." His gun came up. Mission couldn't believe it. His friend pointed the barrel at the Old Crow.

"Wait—" Mission raised a hand.

"Stand back," Rodny said. "I have to do this."

"No!"

His friend's arm stiffened. The barrel was leveled at a defenseless woman in a mechanical chair, the mother to them all, the one who sang them to sleep in their cribs and on their mats, whose voice followed them through their shadowing days and beyond.

Frankie shoved a desk aside and lurched toward Rodny. Allie screamed. Mission's legs coiled with the power of a thousand climbs. He threw himself sideways as the gun roared and flashed. There was a punch to his stomach, a fire in his gut. He crashed to the floor as the gun thundered a second time, the Crow's chair lurching to the side as her hand spasmed.

Mission clutched his stomach. His hands came away sticky and wet.

Lying on his back, he saw the Crow slump over in her chair, a chair that no longer moved. Again, the gun roared. Needlessly. Her body twitched as it was struck. Frankie flew into Rodny, and the two men went tumbling. Boots stormed into the room, summoned by the noise.

Allie was there, crying. She kept her hands on Mission's stomach, pressing so hard, and looked back at the Crow. She wailed for them both.

Mission tasted blood in his mouth. It reminded him of the time Rodny had punched him as a kid, only playing. They'd only ever been playing. Costumes and pretending to be their fathers.

There were boots everywhere. Shiny and black boots on some, scuffed with wear on others. Those who had fought before and those just learning.

Frankie screamed. Boots shuffled. And then Rodny appeared above Mission, his eyes wide with worry. He told him to hang in there. Mission wanted to say he'd try, but the pain in his belly was too great. He couldn't speak. They told him to stay awake, but all he'd ever wanted was to sleep. To not be. To not be a burden to anyone.

"Damn you!" Allie screamed, and it was at him, at Mission, not at Rodny. She blubbered that she loved him, and Mission tried to say he knew. He wanted to tell her that she was right all along. He imagined for a moment the kids they would have, the plot of soil if they combined their holdings, the long uninterrupted rows of corn like lives that stretched out for generations. Generations of people staying close to home, there for each other, doing what they knew best, enjoying being a burden to one another.

He wanted to say all these things and more. Much more. But as Allie bent close and he struggled to form the words, all that came out, a whisper amid the din of boots and shouts, was that today was his birthday.

www.hughhowey.com

A WORD FROM THE AUTHOR

Everyone wants to know where Jules is, who will play her in the film, what's going on with the kids in Silo 17, and I have to admit: I'm as eager as anyone to revisit her. So thank you for suffering these SHIFT books, which are dear to me in a way that few will appreciate. The post apocalyptic genre has a tendency to gloss over the cause of the end-times and to remove those responsible from the equation. Perhaps there's good reason for this. Perhaps the *why* and *how* aren't as exciting as the *what's next?*

I, however, am eager to see those who think they have good reason for causing so much suffering answer to the ones they've inflicted it upon. Long gone are the days when mortals were able to shake their fists at Mount Olympus and expect an answer from cruel gods. Jules, perhaps, will be given that chance.

THIRD SHIFT will wrap this trilogy with a look at Jimmy's time during the fall of Silo 17 and his gradual transformation into the man we come to know as Solo. I'm excited to tell that story. And I look forward to wrapping the overall series up by bringing Donald's world into contact with Juliette's. This third and final act will be entitled DUST, and I'm leaning toward releasing it in small parts, similar to WOOL. I'm undecided. But hey, not knowing is half the fun.

A final note for how awesome you have made my life this past year. It's been a magical ride. There's no way you've gotten as much out of these stories as I've gotten out of our interactions, your emails, your comments, and reviews. I can't thank you enough for making me happier and damned luckier than I have any right to be. I get up and work hard at this every day because of how rewarding you all make it.

Epilogue

Hush my Darling, don't you cry
I'm going to sing you a lullaby
Though I'm far away it seems
I'll be with you in your dreams.

Hush my Darling, go to sleep
All around you angels keep
In the morn and through the day
They will keep your fears at bay.

Sleep my Darling, don't you cry
I'm going to sing you a lullaby

Silo 18

Mission changed out of his work coveralls while Allie readied dinner. He washed his hands, scrubbing the dirt from beneath his fingernails, and watched the mud slide down the drain. The ring on his finger was getting more and more difficult to remove, his knuckles sore and stiff from the hoeing of a planting season.

He soaped his hands and finally managed to work the ring off. Remembering the time he'd lost it down the drain, he set it aside carefully. Allie whistled in the kitchen while she tended the stove. When she cracked the oven, he smelled the pork roast inside. He'd have to say something. They couldn't go buying roasts on no occasion.

His coveralls went into the wash. There were candles on the table when he got back to the kitchen. Lit candles. They were for emergencies, for the times when the fools below switched generators and worked on the busted main. Allie knew this. But before he could say anything about the roast or the candles, or tell her that the bean crop wouldn't be what he'd hoped come harvest, he saw the way she was beaming at him. There was only one thing to be that happy about—but it was impossible.

"No," he said. He couldn't allow himself to believe it.

Allie nodded. There were tears in her eyes. By the time he got to her, they were coursing down her cheeks.

"But our ticket is up," he whispered, holding her against him. She smelled like sweet peppers and sage. He could feel her trembling.

Allie sobbed. Her voice broke from being overfull of joy. "Doc says it happened last month. It was in our window, Mish. We're gonna have a baby."

A surge of relief filled Mission to the brim. Relief, not excitement. Relief that everything was legal, on the up-and-up. He wasn't sure why this is what he felt. He kissed his wife's cheek, salt to go with the pepper and sage. "I love you," he whispered.

"The roast." She pulled away and hurried to the stove. "I was gonna tell you after dinner."

Mission laughed. "You were gonna tell me now or have to explain the candles."

He poured two glasses of water, hands trembling, and set them out while she fixed the plates. The smell of cooked meat made his mouth water. He could anticipate the way the roast would taste like it was already in his mouth. A taste of the future, of what was to come. Like by the table, how he could already see two children, two more mouths to feed. He'd have to find a way to put in another row of corn. Or take that part time delivery job he'd been thinking about, just on weekends.

"Don't let it get cold," Allie said, setting the plates.

They sat and held hands. Mission cursed himself for not putting his ring back on.

"Bless this food and those who fed its roots," Allie said.

"Amen," said Mission. His wife squeezed his hands before letting go and grabbing her utensils.

"You know," she said, cutting into the roast, "if it's a girl, we'll have to name her Allison. Every woman in my family as far back as we can remember has been an Allison."

Mission wondered how far back her family could remember. Be unusual, if they could. The first piece of meat hit his tongue, an explosion of flavors. He chewed and thought on the name. "Allison it is," he said. And he thought that eventually they would call her Allie, too. "But if it's a boy, can we go with Cam?"

"Sure." Allie lifted her glass. "That wasn't your grandfather's name, was it?"

"Hmm? No. I don't know a Cam. I just like the way it sounds."

He picked up his glass of water, studied it a while. Or did he know a Cam? Where did he know that name from? There was something he was supposed to remember, something about the way water gets made, gets purified. But there were pockets of his past shrouded and hidden from him. There were things like the mark on his neck and the scar on his stomach that he couldn't remember coming to be. Everyone had their share of these things, parts of their bygone days they couldn't recall, but Mission more than most. Like his birthday. It drove him crazy that he couldn't remember when his birthday was. What was so hard about that?

All changes, even the most longed for, have their melancholy;
for what we leave behind us is a part of ourselves;
we must die to one life before we can enter another.

-Anatole France

Silo 1

"Sir?"

There was a clatter of bones beneath his feet. Donald stumbled through the dark.

"Can you hear me?"

The haze parted, an eyelid cracking, just like the seal of his pod. A bean. Donald was curled inside that pod like a bean.

"Sir? Are you with me?"

Skin so cold. Donald was sitting up, steam rising from his bare legs. He didn't remember going to sleep. He remembered a doctor, remembered being in his office. Not his office, an airlock. They were talking. People were angry. Now he was being woken up.

"Drink this, sir."

Donald remembered this. He remembered waking over and over, but he didn't remember going to sleep. Just the waking. He took a sip, had to concentrate to make his throat work, had to fight to swallow. A pill. There was supposed to be a pill, but it wasn't offered.

"Sir, we had instructions to wake you."

Instructions. Rules. Protocol. Donald was in trouble again. Troy. Maybe it was that Troy fellow. Who was he? Donald drank as much as he could.

"Very good, sir. We're going to lift you out."

He was in trouble. They only woke him when there was trouble. A catheter was removed, a needle extracted from his arm.

"What did I—?"

He coughed into his fist. His voice was a sheet of tissue paper, thin and fragile. Invisible.

"What is it?" he asked, shouting to form a whisper.

Two men lifted him up and set him into a wheelchair. A third man held it still. There was a soft blanket instead of a paper gown. There was no rustling this time, no itching on his skin.

"We lost one," someone said.

A silo. A silo was gone. It would be Donald's fault again. "Eighteen," he whispered, remembering his last shift.

Two of the men glanced at each other, mouths open.

"Yes," one of them said, awe in his voice. "From Silo Eighteen, sir. We lost her over the hill. We lost contact."

Donald tried to focus on the man. He remembered losing someone over a hill. *Helen.* His wife. They were still looking for her. There was still hope.

"Tell me," he whispered.

"We're not sure how, but one of them made it out of sight."

"A cleaner, sir—"

A cleaner. Donald sank into the chair; his bones were as cold and heavy as stone. It wasn't Helen at all.

"Over the hill—" one said.

"We got a call from Eighteen—"

Donald raised his hand a little, his arm trembling and still half-numb from the sleep. "Wait," he croaked. "One at a time. Why did you wake me?" It hurt to talk. He remembered a hill. A view over a hill.

One of the men cleared his throat. The blanket was tucked up under Donald's chin to stop him from shivering. He hadn't known he was shivering. They were being so reverent with him, so gentle. What was this? He tried to clear his head.

"You told us to wake you—"

"It's protocol—"

Donald's eyes fell to the pod, still steaming as the chill escaped. There was a screen at the base, empty readouts without him in there, just a rising temp. A rising temp and a name. Not his name.

And Donald remembered a conversation. He didn't remember going to sleep, but he remembered a doctor, a man with glasses and an accent telling him how names meant nothing unless that was all we had to go by. Unless we didn't remember each other, didn't cross paths, and then a name was everything.

"Sir?"

"Who am I?" he asked, reading the little screen, not understanding. This wasn't him. "Why did you wake me?"

"You told us to, Mr. Thurman."

The blanket was wrapped snugly around his shoulders. The chair was turned. They were treating him with respect, like he had authority. The wheels on this chair did not squeak at all.

"It's okay, sir. Your head will clear soon."

He didn't know these people. They didn't know him.

"The doctor will clear you for duty."

Nobody knew anyone.

"Right this way."

And then anyone could be anybody.

"Through here."

Until it didn't matter who was in charge. One who might do what was needed, another who might do what was right.

"Very good."

One name as good as any other.

In memory of Michael Fry